RANDOM PSYCHIC - A SHADE OF MIND - BOOK 1

D.N. LEO

A SHADE OF MIND
by D.N Leo

RANDOM PSYCHIC
FOREVER MORTAL
ELUSIVE BEINGS
IMPERFECT DIVINE

>>>SERIES HOME PAGE<<<

CHAPTER 1

Hate leaves ugly scars, love leaves beautiful ones.
Mignon McLaughlin, The Second Neurotic's Notebook, 1966

She stared at the last three seconds of her life.

A red double-decker full of passengers was racing straight at her, and she couldn't do anything but stare at it.

Like the traffic and everything else surrounding it, the bus seemed to move in slow motion, but Madeline was more than certain that it was zooming in full speed in reality.

The bus was going to crush her the same way the kidnap and ransom ordeal had cut short Jo's life.

Jo was like her sister. They had grown up together, but they might not grow old together.

Madeline kept staring at the bus. It was real. It was enormous. And her psychic ability didn't seem to help at all—if she did have such ability.

Five seconds ago, Madeline had seen it—the haunting blue dot hovering in the air, giving her guidance. She couldn't believe her eyes. She was a psychic after all. The blue dot glared at her and blinked. *That's unusual,* she had thought. It had been three days that she'd stalked this place, and now her psychic ability had finally decided to kick in. *About damn time!*

She could save Jo now, and her life would be back to the way it was. Not that her life had been spectacular, but it was much better than her current situation.

The second blue dot appeared, blinking at her. She gazed at the dots, and then they were no longer blinking. They weren't blue, either, but a bright yellow.

And they came with sound.

Honking.

Shouting.

She blinked. They weren't her psychic blue dots but the headlights of a double-decker racing at her in full speed.

She glanced around. In a blur of motion, she realized she had just stepped out in front of ongoing traffic in the middle of a busy road in the center of London.

She now stood in her reality and froze.

CHAPTER 2

Someone grabbed Madeline's arm and pulled her back onto the sidewalk. The double-decker zoomed past, and the other cars kept moving. If it had been New York, she would have stirred up a hideous bout of road rage. Madeline was still dazed. She turned around and looked at the man who had just saved her life.

"Are you okay?"

"Thank you," she automatically said and immediately realized that those words she kept in her vocabulary inventory didn't exactly answer the man's question.

Then Madeline shook her head. *Focus. Stay strong. You're Jo's only hope,* she scolded herself. She turned toward the man, who was still looking at her with concern.

"I'm fine. Thank you. I'm sorry. The jetlag is killing me. And apparently, I was looking the wrong way." She gestured toward the traffic and smiled. "Madeline. I'm from New York." She reached her hand out for a handshake.

"Peter. I'm from . . . here . . . apparently." He fumbled

with his briefcase, swapping it to his left hand so that he could respond to Madeline's greeting.

Madeline pointed at the building across the road. "I'm looking for LeBlanc Pharmaceuticals. But I think I've got the wrong address. That building looks more like military barracks than business headquarters."

Peter arched an eyebrow, looking Madeline up and down.

"I'm a journalist. I'm writing a business column about one of their new products. Is there a problem?" Madeline asked.

"Oh, no. No problem at all. Nobody has any problem with the LeBlancs."

Madeline smiled and waited for the next part of Peter's speech, but it never came. Instead, he shrugged. "Well, to be honest, even the locals know almost nothing about them. I'm sorry I can't help you. But I can certainly show you around if it does any good. And the I around the corner is one of London's hot spots. I'm sure it will help cure your jet lag."

Madeline smiled but cursed on the inside. Peter was a decent-looking man. She hadn't been in a serious relationship for a while—not that no one was interested in her, but her situation was too complicated to let anyone into her life. Still, it was nice to be hit on occasionally.

She was tall, slim, and attractive enough, but Madeline didn't consider herself pretty. She had a slightly long, oval face, big brown eyes, a generous mouth with full lips, and a dimple on her left cheek. A sea of brunette curls wrapped around her shoulders.

A hot cup of coffee was tempting, but now was not a good time. "I'm sorry. I've got to get this done, or my boss will be very unhappy. Thanks for the offer, Peter. Maybe next time." Madeline waved her gloveless hand goodbye and scurried away, shivering in the winter chill.

She glanced at the reflection on the shop window and saw that the smile on Peter's face had been replaced by a strange look.

She wouldn't be mistaken. She had seen that look several times. It was the look of a predator who had just lost his prey.

Instead of going straight home, she turned to the opposite direction and headed toward a crowed shopping center.

CHAPTER 3

*H*ours later, throwing her light backpack over her shoulders, Madeline headed toward a small apartment on a back street in Knightsbridge. Rows of terrace houses that curved along a tree-lined street looked invitingly at her. The black gothic-styled light poles and street fences accentuated the beautiful blend of modern and classic London.

She normally adored and admired the architecture. But right now, Madeline was cursing the amount of money she had to pay to stay in Knightsbridge on such short notice.

There—she saw those blue dots again.

It had been a secret she'd only told Jo, and Jo called it her psychic ability. After the incident in the bush that both Madeline and Jo didn't want to remember, Madeline had appeared to be able to see people's *minds*—or at least she thought that's what it was.

Sometimes it came from those she had been in contact with. That was how Jo speculated she was able to track down a missing person. Sometimes it randomly came from a stranger when they directed their thoughts at her. Other times, she had absolutely no explanation of where the dots came from. She wasn't a mind reader—she didn't know what the thoughts were about. She just saw them as the blue dots.

Ironically, her randomly found ability only worked when she didn't need it, like when it had led her in front of a fast approaching bus.

The dots hovered in front of her and then moved toward the alley leading to Hyde Park. After the near-fatal encounter with the bus, Madeline didn't think it was wise to follow the psychic specks anymore. She ignored them and headed home.

~

HER CELL PHONE buzzed as soon as she entered her apartment. She picked up the phone and kicked the door closed.

"Madeline," she answered while searching for the light switch on the wall.

At the other end of the line, a male voice croaked, "I miss you. It's been a few days. What have you got for me?"

"Zen, I almost got hit by a bus trying to get to the door of LeBlanc Pharmaceuticals. Their premises are guarded like a military barracks. Seriously, I'd have a better chance of running through the gates of Buckingham Palace to the Queen's private chamber than breaking into the front yard of that building."

"That's why I sent you there, honey. We can't compete with the LeBlancs using weapons, money, or manpower. Your little gift is just what we need."

Madeline finally found the light switch. She flicked it on and strode toward the fireplace. Her teeth were never going to stop chattering if she didn't get a fire going.

"I don't have any gift, Zen. You know I can barely

operate a computer let alone hunt down a computer geek and ask him questions about an avatar."

"I saw the games you played with Jo, Madeline. Don't bluff with me."

Madeline closed her eyes. *Damn.* Jo made her play guessing games just to prove that Madeline's psychic ability was real. Jo believed in it more than she did. Since Jo was doing research on a new simulation game, Madeline thought it would be fun to help out. Now those games were biting her in the backside.

"Look, Zen, it's been days, and I haven't been able to get inside. You have to give me more information than just 'look for a White Knight.'"

"But that's all I have!" Zen screamed though the phone. She could hear his heavy breathing and his swallow to suppress his anger.

She lowered her voice. "If you let me talk to Jo, we could figure something out."

"You want to talk to her? Okay." Zen turned on the video phone. He grabbed Jo's hair and smashed her face onto the screen of the phone. "Do you see her now? Talk away. You girls can figure things out, right?"

Madeline caught a glimpse of Zen's face, which was burning red with fury. Jo's eyes were dazed, and her forehead was bruised. Jo bit her lips and looked into the screen. Madeline knew Jo wouldn't cry.

"You hurt her, you bastard. You told me you wouldn't hurt her if I found your stupid avatar!" Madeline roared.

"But you found *nothing*!" Zen screamed.

CHAPTER 4

"*H*e didn't hurt me, Madeline. I tried to run and fell down the stairs. Should have taken my stupid heels off." Jo smiled weakly.

A tear rolled down Madeline's cheek. Jo was barely five foot two, and she always wore those impossibly high heels. Madeline couldn't understand why she was so conscious about her height. Jo was gorgeous. She was a brilliant computer game designer, but no one could peg her as a nerd. Madeline wiped her tear and smiled back.

"You sure you're okay?"

"I'm fine. You take care of yourself, Madeline."

"I can't get the blue dots to work, Jo. Can you tell me what the game is about? What am I looking for?"

Jo was about to say something, but Zen yanked her off the phone. "All you have to do is to find out who plays with Jo using the name White Knight. You've seen the game—and the player. You should be able to tell who the guy is in real life. I told you he works for the LeBlancs and has been playing from that building. You don't have to go in. Just wait him out."

"Do you understand that LeBlanc Pharmaceuticals is a global company that employs millions of people?"

"But I gave you the *precise* location!"

"I told you, it's like a military barrack. I used my journalist credentials to ask for an interview with their PR department..."

"And?"

"The waiting list is a month."

"I don't have a month. I give you three days."

"It's not possible..."

"I don't give a shit. If I don't get this done in time, I'll be dead. But I'm not going down alone. I can guarantee you that. I'll send you more info as soon as I have it. But three days is all the time you've got."

Zen hung up.

Madeline slid down to the floor and curled up next to the sofa. She let the tears fall freely. She could fall apart right here, right now. Nobody knew, and nobody cared. Jo was her family—the only family Madeline had ever known. She had taken her in and had shared her family with Madeline unconditionally. Jo's parents had never once asked Madeline about her own family—they knew she didn't have one. Otherwise, she would've had to tell them that she had come in a basket, abandoned on the front porch of some random house.

Her teeth chattered, and her body shook with the chill. She couldn't remember the last time she'd eaten or slept.

At the corner of the room, the fireplace stood cold and empty. She had forgotten to start the fire.

A shadow hovered at the window and tripped over the potted plant at the front door, but Madeline had drifted to sleep and heard nothing.

A piece of paper slid under her door.

A crash woke Madeline. She jumped up to her feet, panting.

Then she let out a sigh of relief. She had kicked the side table in her sleep, and the vase on top of the table had crashed to the floor.

Madeline checked the clock. She must have passed out for the night. It was just past five in the morning. She glanced out the window without any hope of seeing the winter sun at this hour. Madeline went to the kitchen to make herself a strong mug of coffee and to find something with which to clean up the broken vase.

A short moment later, she settled in front of her computer and stared at the mountain of documentation she had researched about LeBlanc Pharmaceuticals.

Secrets.

That was the conclusion she had drawn. Not that she couldn't find any information. On the contrary, there was too much information. Ten years of experience in journalism had taught her that the information about the LeBlancs was only a facade. Even the underground information revealed nothing about the company that they didn't want the public to know.

The LeBlanc family was filthy rich—and extremely private.

Madeline had to congratulate herself after hours of searching. She found one picture of the current head of the family, Ciaran LeBlanc. One lousy picture. The picture must have come from a very keen stalker. It was taken from a distance, and the scene it showed was reflected on a traffic monitoring mirror in a car park.

Judging by the proportion of the cars and guards around him, Madeline speculated that Ciaran was tall and well-built, but on the slender side.

Young, she mused, and maybe long hair. The picture

was so distorted that Madeline wasn't sure she would have recognized Ciaran if she met him in the flesh.

She drew imaginary lines with her finger around Ciaran's face, trying to make out the part that the poor quality image didn't catch.

Then she glanced at the corner of the door, on the floor, and saw the note.

Madeline picked the note up.

It read, "Hyde Park."

CHAPTER 5

*M*adeline stretched for her morning run and winced at how stiff her body felt after slacking off for a week. Hyde Park was just around the corner from her place. *Had Zen wanted to tip her off as to where the LeBlancs lived?* She doubted that.

There were residential areas in Hyde Park, but she couldn't imagine the LeBlancs in these apartments, regardless of how exclusive they were. Madeline speculated that members of the LeBlanc family lived in castles in secret highlands.

She jiggled a container of self-defense spray in her pocket to ensure it was secured and within easy reach, then headed to the park.

The fog was as thick as clouds. Madeline could hardly see more than ten feet in front of her. She kept to the left, but then by habit drifted over to the right. Suddenly right in front of her, a man emerged from the fog like a warrior. Late thirties. Tall. At least six foot three, she would guess, with a slender build and well-toned muscles covered attractively in fair English skin. His thick, black hair almost touched his shoulders. His strong face, the face of a dark angel, looked straight ahead before it registered the coming motion. His eyes . . . Madeline was sure that it was his eyes that caused such an electrifying reaction in her body. Dark, smoky gray eyes. Intense, captivating, and striking.

Because Madeline had spent so much time evaluating the beauty of the human being in front of her, she didn't have any time to adjust her speed or steer herself away from the imminent collision. She would have been knocked off her feet and landed on her backside if he hadn't grabbed her.

"Goddamn it, don't you look when you run, Ciaran?"

The words were out before she could edit them. She had called his name, which meant she had to think with lightning speed right now to explain herself—to explain that she was not a stalker. Her thoughts ran rampant. She could tell him it wasn't him she was after, she wanted his company. No. She didn't want his company, she needed the guy who worked in his company. Hmm . . . but that wouldn't explain how she knew his name. Maybe she should tell him she's a psychic? No again. That would be a lie, and it wouldn't go down well. Her thoughts tangled in a mushy mess, and she felt as if her face was on fire.

Ciaran released Madeline after a swivel to balance the running momentum so that they both regained their footing. "Excuse me!" he said.

"Sorry, it was my fault. I should have kept right—no, I mean left."

"Is that an offense to run on a wrong side of a pedestrian path in a public park in New York?"

She wanted to swoon with the sexy accent, but her suspicion had gotten a better judgment of her. Madeline narrowed her eyes. "How do you know I'm from New York?"

"Your accent gave it away. I have a lot of business dealings in New York. I can tell." Ciaran grinned.

Her heart skipped a beat when she saw that grin. *For pity's sake, you're thirty-three, not a teenager, Madeline. Focus.*

Ciaran drank from his bottle water and sat down on the bench. "I don't think my name is written on my forehead."

"Talk to your PR department. I'm the reporter who's been bugging them for the past few days to get an interview. Of course I know your name." That was lame, she thought. Ciaran didn't have a public profile, and she couldn't even get a decent picture of him. But she couldn't think of anything else, so she settled with the statement.

Ciaran nodded politely, and waited.

"Oh, I'm Madeline Roux, from *The Trumpet*." Madeline reached her hand out for a handshake.

"*The Trumpet?*"

She didn't need to look at Ciaran's face to see his expression. "Oh, we're certainly not the *New York Times* or anything . . ."

"I beg your pardon. I didn't mean to offend . . ." He stood up quickly from the bench to return the handshake before she withdrew her hand.

Madeline laughed. "You have to do a lot better than that to offend me. We're young, small, and not a mainstream magazine. Of course you've never heard of us."

Ciaran smiled. "How off-stream are you?"

"Well, let's say we're just a bit quirky in our approach to serious issues."

Ciaran murmured, "Ah, interesting! So you don't just blow the whistle, you blow the whole magnificent trumpet to the glory!"

Madeline laughed. "You've got it, Ciaran!"

She suddenly realized that she hadn't laughed for days. It felt good. But it was much too friendly. Madeline tilted her head to look behind Ciaran. He turned, looking in the same direction.

"What are you looking for?"

"Bodyguards."

Ciaran looked at Madeline blankly. Then he just laughed.

"You think I'd have bodyguards with me when I go running? Who do you think I am? A prince?"

"Practically," Madeline muttered.

"I beg your pardon?" His smile faded.

"What do you expect people to think? Your family isn't media friendly. Your company has more security than the military. Nobody knows anything about your family. It is more difficult to approach you than it is to make an appointment to see the Queen!"

"Well, that's because the Queen has to answer to her people. We don't have to answer to anyone."

"Or you'd have everyone answer to you?"

Ciaran lowered his voice. "We have money. But we don't bribe or bully anyone. I don't care for my family being judged because we want our privacy." Ciaran jammed his hands in his pockets, waiting for Madeline's response.

She cursed herself. "I'm sorry. It's just been very hard to get in touch with you. I mean with your PR department. It's almost impossible, and my boss isn't happy at all about my progress."

Ciaran nodded. "What did *The Trumpet* want to talk to our PR department about? You came all the way from New York—it couldn't be a minor issue."

"Nothing serious, really. I suggested the topic. LeBlanc

Pharmaceuticals is a very successful business. I'm sure the media has made the most of what they could. But for me, behind that business success is always the people. I always find your family . . . intriguing."

Ciaran smiled. "You think we have something to hide?"

"No, I think you have a lot to show. I'd like to have a bit of what you're willing to show."

Ciaran paused for a brief moment then nodded. "So is it my family or my family's business that you're interested in?"

She looked into Ciaran's eyes. They were intense now, deep gray and mysteriously serious.

"Both."

He shook his head. "You have only one option."

"Your family."

A slight smile crossed Ciaran's face. "Then you can interview me. I will represent my family. Would tomorrow night be convenient? Over dinner?"

"What? Of course! Dinner?"

"That's the only time I can manage."

Madeline nodded.

Ciaran smiled. "Seven p.m. at One Hyde Park. I'm looking forward to it. Goodbye for now, Madeline." Ciaran nodded a goodbye and turned to walk away.

"Why? Your family has never talked to the media before."

Ciaran turned around, sending Madeline a look that made her stomach quiver. "Simply because I'd like to see more of you!" he said.

Then he walked away and disappeared into the fog.

adeline's internal clock woke her in the morning—it seemed she had adjusted to the time difference. She didn't have many hours of sleep, but they were good and solid hours, enough to get her going and be prepared. Tonight was her chance to end this and put her life back to normal.

Was that all she wanted with the dinner? Had she thought about Ciaran at all?

She got off the bed, giving herself a mental slap whenever her brain wandered in Ciaran's direction. She needed to stay focused and plan for the night.

She should have chosen the business rather than the family when Ciaran gave her the options. But the man headed the family *and* ran the business. He could give her the exact information she needed. If she had gone with the business option, then she might have ended up with one of the minions whose job was to withhold information from her.

Madeline made herself a cup of coffee and stopped that

stream of thought. There was no point rationalizing a past action that she couldn't reverse anyway.

Her response to Ciaran in the park hadn't been optimal. But she was a woman, and his physical attraction was undeniable. *Hell, he was like a magnet!* Mental slap.

Madeline tucked at her hair, pulling it back into a ponytail and putting herself into active working mode. Her phone rang. Paul's voice squeaked through from the other end of the line when Madeline picked up.

"Here you are, still on the planet. Thank God. You can't just go poof and let me handle everything, Maddie!"

Paul was co-editor with Madeline at *The Trumpet*. His task was to add a feminine touch to the magazine. Balance the scales, he always said, as Madeline had made the magazine quite 'boyish.' Paul was a decent writer and a good guy in the industry, as far as Madeline concerned.

"A girl is entitled to a vacation, Paul!"

"I'm so glad that you finally realize you're a girl! Yes, you can take a vacation. But you have to give me some notice in advance of more than, say, half an hour! Also, I can take care for your half-finished stories, but not your half-eaten slop, half-finished carrot rubber, and half-decent boyfriend."

"First, the slop is homemade lasagna, and you're lucky to have half of it. Second, the carrot cake is from Jo's brother's one-of-a-kind bakery, and he specifically baked it for me. So you're welcome to have it, and I'll thank them on your behalf. Third, Stephen is not a half-decent man. He's better than a lot of guys I know."

"Oh, so Stephen is your boyfriend now, is he?"

"Who were you talking about?"

"Not Stephen, apparently! A bold guy. Shuffling through your desk like a thief. Took off when I called out.

Be careful, Maddie. I think you might have a stalker . . . and that's a best-case scenario."

Madeline felt a pinch of worry. A dozen what-if scenarios flew through her mind. "Are you okay?" she asked Paul. "I'm sorry if this worries you."

"No, I'm all right," Paul said.

"You want me to call Stephen? He's a cop. He could do something about this."

"No, no," Madeline assured him. "I can handle this. Give me a few days. I'll sort it out, I promise. Let me know if anything else happens. Hey . . . how about you work from home for a few days?"

Paul chuckled. "Really, Maddie?"

"Yeah, really," Madeline said. "Just do that for me, will you? I'll talk to you later. I'll explain more. Everything. Okay?"

Paul reluctantly agreed and hung up the phone.

Madeline called Zen. He switched on the video phone when he picked up the call. His sleazy smile flashed on the screen.

"Miss me?"

"You don't have to sniff around my workplace and freak out other people. I said I'd get the information for you, and I will." Madeline fumed.

The smile disappeared from Zen's face. "I didn't snoop around no place. Who else knows about this?"

A missed step, damn! Slow down, she warned herself.

"No, I'm just annoyed, that's all. I have a few unkind readers sending nasty notes to my paper, that's all."

"Your job sucks. Poking your nose into other people's business—you'll end up with something as big as a bomb or as little a bullet. They're both lethal, though! What have you got for me?"

"Ah . . . not much yet. Is White Knight a game or a character?

"It's an avatar. Jesus Christ! Don't you know anything about games?"

"No, not really. I don't even know exactly how to get the information. Even if I should get inside the LeBlanc premises, you want me just to go around asking who plays White Knight?"

Madeline could picture Zen wanting to knock his head against the wall to quell his frustration. *Maybe it was her head that he wanted to whack.* She chuckled on the inside and kept a straight face. Playing dumb was working for her at this point, so she kept at it.

Zen calmly explained, "No, don't ask directly, and don't alarm any one. All you have to do is to tell them that one computer within their premises was used to play an interactive game. Make it up. Say the game was illegal or whatever. Don't say anything about White Knight at this stage. I need a list of the real names of those who played games from that building. If you can narrow it down to the one guy who plays as White Knight, that's ideal. But I understand it might be difficult. Got it?"

Madeline nodded.

"When can I expect some results?"

"Come on, you only gave me Hyde Park. That's a residential address, not the business headquarters. How am I supposed to . . ."

"What? I didn't give you the address. I didn't know the address. Who tipped you? Who else knows about this?" Zen's face started to burn with anger.

Fuck! This is a total fuck-up. Who wrote the note? She searched frantically in her mind for an answer but found nothing.

"What happened? You better fucking tell me!" Zen yelled into the phone.

"I . . . I was . . ."

"Tell me!" Zen's demonic voice threatened to rip open the phone.

CHAPTER 7

*T*he ceiling-high, double-steel door automatically slid open when Ciaran approached, revealing a vast lush office with glass windows opening to the endless horizon of the city. Before the door closed, Lindsay called from behind, "Ciaran!" and trailed into the office with a stack of paper in his hands.

Ciaran turned around. "Yes, Lindsay, did I forget to sign something?"

Lindsay Freeman was in his late thirties and had been Ciaran's right-hand man as long as Ciaran had been in business. As they were of similar age, Ciaran could talk to Lindsay almost about anything. They were good friends, and Ciaran trusted Lindsay to be the face of the business when it came to dealing with outsiders.

"You'll want to take a look at this," Lindsay said and put a computer disc on the desk.

Ciaran glanced at the disc. "Gate security? Shouldn't Robert be handling this?" He slid the disc into the computer.

"I just checked things over, and this caught my eye."

Ciaran shook his head. "You can't keep an eye on everything. Robert's a very capable man."

"No doubt about that. But I'll sleep better checking everything this week because you're here."

"I don't want to be the cause of your sleep deprivation. By the way, how are Liz and Anna?"

"Enjoying their vacation at a warm beach in Bali now." Lindsay grinned. "Anna finished her exams with good grades and wanted a vacation before entering high school."

Ciaran stopped looking at the computer monitor. "You're saying you let your wife and daughter go on a vacation by themselves because I'm here this week?"

Lindsay laughed. "Come on. I know your schedule, and work is important, Ciaran. They decided on the vacation on a whim. It's hardly my fault."

Ciaran shook his head. "When they kick you out of the house, you aren't going sleep on my couch."

The secretary knocked on the door and walked in with a tray. She put the coffee on the desk. "Double shot, no cream for you, Ciaran. Double cream for you, Lindsay." She put a plate of four small cookies on the desk. "Mom made these and insisted I take them to work for you, Ciaran. She does this every week. She thinks you're in the office nine to five, five days a week." She smiled. "I ate your cookies every other week. But today, they're all yours."

Ciaran grinned. "Butterscotch. My favorite. Thank you, Lily." He reached out for a cookie and his gaze lighted on Lily's hand. Ciaran dropped the cookies back to the plate. He stood up, walked around his desk, and kissed Lily on the cheek. "Congratulations, Sam is a very lucky guy."

Lily smiled and twirled her engagement ring around her finger. "Thank you. It was last week. We're very happy . . . Well, I'd better let you go back to work." She nodded a goodbye and exited the room. Ciaran grabbed the desk phone and ordered flowers to be sent to Lily's address. Then he looked up and saw Lindsay shaking his head.

"You haven't seen me doing this before?" Ciaran arched an eyebrow.

"I only say this as a friend. It's been such a long time since . . ."

"Don't start," Ciaran cut in with a voice so low that it almost sounded like a growl. Then he pointed at the computer monitor. "What did you want me to look at here?" As soon as Ciaran finished his question, he saw the answer. On the screen was Madeline in front of the LeBlanc Pharmaceuticals, walking right in front of a double-decker.

"You see that?" Lindsay asked.

Ciaran nodded. "Yes, I know her. That's Madeline Roux. She's a journalist from New York."

"I'm not talking about her. I'm talking about the guy."

Ciaran frowned, looking at the man dragging Madeline out of the way of the bus. "He's no random pedestrian. From this angle, he must have been stalking right at our door steps. We got the scanner data on that, right?"

"Yep, that's where the ass-kicker stuff is," Lindsay muttered.

Ciaran pulled out the keyboard and typed in the command and codes to pull up the scanner data. On the screen was the x-ray scanned data of a five hundred meter perimeter outside the gate. Ciaran was about to ask something, but Lindsay said in anticipation, "Robert kept a very tight lid on the scanner. We know it's not strictly legal. You don't have to be the only one to keep an eye on everything!" Lindsay smiled to himself as he had evened the scores with Ciaran.

Ciaran's smile faded as he stared at the monitor.

CHAPTER 8

*T*he room got colder by the second. The screen of the phone in front of Madeline felt as if it was going to explode. Her head wanted to evaporate.

She knew Zen was going to do something bad. *Think fast!*

"I was doing some research . . ." she said.

"Don't you fucking lie to me again . . ." Zen grabbed the phone and walked toward a door.

"I've got it. I've got the access . . ." she spoke too fast and stuttered.

Zen walked into another room and tilted the phone so that Madeline could see that Jo was tied to a bed. "You know why she doesn't scream? Because nobody can hear her from down here. No one can save her but you."

Tears streamed down Jo's face. She looked so tired and dazed with drugs.

Madeline wiped at the tears streaming down on her face as well. "I'm sorry. I'm so sorry, Zen. I'm not lying to you about anything. Please don't hurt her. Yes, I've done some research, and I got some information about a possible place of residence for the LeBlancs. I might be able to get an interview tonight with my journalist credentials. Please don't hurt her!"

Zen tore off Jo's shirt.

Jo cried. But she did not beg.

"Please don't hurt her. I'll do whatever I can tonight to get you the information. I'll get you the list. No one else knows about this, I swear . . ." Madeline cried.

Zen climbed onto the bed. He grabbed Jo and hitched up her hips.

Madeline screamed into the phone. "Please, don't! I'll get you the list."

Zen turned slowly to the phone. "Then you'd better keep your promise. I'll call you tomorrow morning."

Zen reached out and turned off the call.

As soon as the phone was off, Madeline slid down to the floor and wept. She had never felt that helpless in her life.

~

IN CIARAN'S OFFICE, Lindsay pointed at the computer monitor. The video showed an enlarged picture of the brief case the man was carrying.

"What's he doing carrying a silencer and hanging around our front gate. I've checked the surveillance data. He's only been there this week. I think he's waiting for you, Ciaran."

"Only you and Robert know my schedule. There are much more convenient ways to get to me than lurking at the gate. Plus, I don't use that gate. If he's waiting for me there, then he's an amateur. Not worth our trouble."

"More convenient ways? Like at home? Man, Robert'd be offended hearing that!"

Ciaran nodded. "Yes, at home, wherever it is," he muttered. "I'm having dinner with Madeline tonight at One Hyde Park."

"You what? Holy shit. She's a reporter. She must be a corporate spy. They're the same gang. The guy stalked the gate, and the girl stalked you at home."

"I don't think they're in the same group. He's her adversary."

Ciaran rewound the clip. "Pay attention to the handle of his briefcase. See that? He slid the knife out an inch. Probably tried to take her hostage or make her walk to a quiet corner and do whatever he intended to do to her."

Ciaran enhanced the image on his computer. "He didn't expect that Madeline would want to shake hands. That forced him change the briefcase to his left hand."

"But if he'd wanted to kill her, why didn't he just let her get run over by the bus?" Lindsay asked.

"Too many variables. The bus might brake in time, or she might have been able to get out of the way by herself. Or the accident might not have been fatal. If he wanted to kill her, then he would want to do it himself. Maybe he just wanted to capture her."

"But why didn't he follow her afterward?"

"He might have. Not right away because it would be too obvious."

"I'll send Robert to the apartment for your dinner tonight then."

"We're good friends, but I don't intend to have dinner with Robert tonight."

"Ciaran!"

Ciaran laughed. "Okay. I'll be careful. You can tell

Robert, but I don't want him to hang too close. It's only a dinner. You think I can't handle a girl?"

"All right. I'll call him now," Lindsay said and exited the room. Ciaran rewound the footage and watched again.

CHAPTER 9

*F*ive minutes to seven. Madeline approached the corner of a series of luxurious apartments. She had no idea which one was actually One Hyde Park, nor did she know the exact number of the apartment.

What an idiot! She turned around the corner to the street front, and there he was, standing next to a marble pole at the entrance to a building, smiling at her.

When they closed the distance, Ciaran frowned. Madeline winced. She must look like crap after her crying marathon. A concerned expression crossed Ciaran's face briefly and then disappeared.

"It was inconsiderate of me not giving you the exact address yesterday. So I thought I should wait for you at the entrance. You look beautiful."

She loved his accent, but she knew a dig when she heard it. She was in black jeans, a deep gray turtleneck, and a long red leather jacket. Yes, the red leather jacket was respectable, given what she could stuff in her emergency travel bag. But what she wore was in no way compatible with the ten-thousand-dollar-minimum outfit on him.

Jo's image was still fresh in her mind, and Zen's voice still echoed in her head. *Oh hell!* She just realized that she'd forgotten to put her makeup on, and she was still wearing her ponytail.

"Madeline?"

"Huh?"

"What's the matter?"

"What? Oh . . . I'm sorry. I'm just very tired. . ." Madeline rubbed at her eyes.

She hated herself at the moment. What happened earlier had knocked all the wits out of her.

Ciaran looked at her, his eyes pausing on her face for a second. He was skilled, she thought. Before the gaze became an awkward moment, he reached out, wrapping his arm around her shoulders, protectively and friendly.

"Come on, let's get some food into you. It always does the trick."

Ciaran led Madeline through the entrance of a gigantic door, via a long hallway that had thick carpets, marble floors, and several pieces of contemporary artwork and into a so-called 'apartment.' Apartment was too humble of a word to describe what she saw, but given her mental state right now, she had to settle for the term.

At the door, Ciaran took his coat off, hanging it in a small cloakroom snugged in the corner. Then he took Madeline's jacket. There was no sign of anyone else in the apartment. There was only his coat and her jacket, cozily hung on fancy hooks.

Madeline glanced at the living room as the grandeur swept over her. She was in no way dressed for such a place, but she kept her poker face. She had a job to do.

The room opened to the city view via glass walls. A dining table was located in the middle of the room. Leather sofas curved cozily in corner. A long glass cabinet containing expensive wine and spirits sat in another corner.

This isn't a home, she observed.

Ciaran shifted a chair out for Madeline to sit down. He walked quickly to the counter of the open kitchen. Noticing her gaze, Ciaran turned around, giving her a big grin.

"You needn't worry. I didn't cook. The food comes from the best kitchen, however. Delivered just ten minutes ago."

"This is how you live?" Madeline gestured widely at the apartment. "Eating takeout by yourself? You don't even have a TV in here. What do you do after work?"

"Pity me!" He smiled again.

The wonderful grin was still on his face when he opened a bottle of red wine. She didn't want to guess the price tag.

"I'll let it breathe a bit."

He turned to the covered plates on the counter and lifted the lids.

"I'm not by myself tonight, am I? You'd make a good companion. I think you'd approve of this excellent menu." Ciaran paused and pretended to scowl. "You didn't expect a full-on banquet, did you?"

Madeline laughed. "I'm not very selective when it comes to food, so you're doing just fine!" She left her chair and helped him to fetch the food and bring it to the table.

They set up the table and started their dinner. The interview began casually. Madeline asked questions that she hated herself for asking because they weren't good enough for even the weather channels or the morning talk shows.

They nearly finished the dinner. Ciaran sipped his wine and looked at Madeline over the rim of the glass.

"So what is it about my family that you really want to know?"

Madeline gave a small pause, then pushed on. "Where do you *actually* live? And don't say it's classified. You're not an FBI agent."

Ciaran laughed. "I can see you've got your real reporter hat back. I thought you'd turned into a robot when I saw you early tonight."

Ciaran paused and focused on Madeline's eyes. "What happened?"

The smile had gone from Ciaran's face. "You have circles under your eyes, and you look as if you spent the entire day crying."

Madeline rubbed absently at her eyes. "I asked the question first." Madeline stared at Ciaran, saying nothing.

Ciaran gave in. "I don't live here. I don't live anywhere for a long time. I travel a lot for business."

Ciaran looked at Madeline for a long moment. This time, he let it grow into an uncomfortable moment. "Now it's my turn to ask a question. What happened to you today that made you cry?"

"I'm interviewing *you*—I get to ask the questions. You agreed to it."

Ciaran calmly stared. "My turf, my rules. I agreed to the interview. I didn't agree to not ask you questions."

"I don't like this. I don't like the setting. I don't like your tone. I don't like your questions. Hell, I don't even like *my* questions. Let's end the interview here. Thank you for your time." Madeline stood up, heading toward the cloakroom.

Ciaran grabbed her elbow. "Wait." When she shrugged him off, he immediately released her and raised up his arms apologetically. "I apologize. It was rude of me to ask you that question. It was inappropriate."

Madeline paused.

"Could we finish the dinner properly, please? I'll answer your questions in the meantime."

Madeline hesitated.

"We still have the dessert. Don't make me eat it by myself." He lowered his voice. "It's a cheesecake. Dark, rich Belgium chocolate with a hint of chili, topped with strawberries, and a touch of . . ."

"Okay, okay, we'll have it!" She swaggered back to her chair. When Ciaran sat down, she shifted, inhaled, exhaled, and started the rant.

"Okay, I'm not interested in your family, your private matters, or your business. A friend of mine developed a computer game with some very special technology. She believes that her program has been hacked by someone using a computer located in your London headquarters. She doesn't have the evidence. So that's why I'm here. To help a friend. I have no proof of the game stealing, nor do I have any authority in this matter. I just need the names of your employees who might have used your equipment to hack my friend's game."

Madeline breathed heavily after the long speech that she had given without even pausing for punctuation. Lying felt horrible. But she had a job to do. Jo's life was at stake.

Ciaran looked at Madeline blankly for a second and cocked an eyebrow. "Is that all?"

Madeline nodded.

Ciaran stood up, heading toward the cloakroom. "Then let's go."

"Go where? Why now?" Madeline followed obediently without even realizing it.

"I won't be here tomorrow, so we have to do this now. I can't reveal the names of my employees who play computer games. Privacy policies. I don't care if they play games. However, I don't like my employees using work equipment to play interactive games with outsiders. That could potentially weaken the system and risk us being hacked. I'd like to think that there's no one playing any games from our operating systems."

They exited the elevator and walked down a long, shiny hallway from the foyer to approach the parking lot. Large screens were mounted on the walls, the sound muted and subtitles scrolling across the bottoms. Out of the corner of her eye, Madeline saw a familiar image flash on a screen. She stopped and watched.

The breaking news was about the unidentified dead body of a man in his mid-thirties found floating in the river. The image of Peter stared back at Madeline. She stared at the photo of the man who had saved her life a day ago. She didn't realize it, but a tear rolled down her face.

"Do you know this man?" Ciaran asked.

She shook her head. "Do you?"

Ciaran gazed into Madeline's eyes. "No," he answered. Then he wrapped his arm around her waist and led her along the corridor toward the entrance to the lot.

He lied, she mused.

CHAPTER 10

*H*alf an hour later, Ciaran parked his car at the side entrance of the headquarters. Madeline noticed he always had his arm around her back to support, lead, or guide her. A primal protective gesture, Madeline thought. She caught the scent of him—natural, spicy, and masculine.

She didn't know what the scent of masculinity was, but at the moment, that was the only word she could find that fit.

She noted the way his Adam's apple moved when he spoke and the exquisite sound produced by the throat that she could easily spend a lifetime exploring. She loved the way he loosened his tie and yanked it off his collar, the way the corner of his mouth quirked when he made a joke, and the way his eyes twinkled. The emotions she saw in those striking gray eyes were genuine.

She wasn't sure at all about her psychic ability, but she was damn sure that her years spent in a relationship drought had led her close to being a slut.

Close.

She had never acted on her need and desire, although she knew she was entitled to. But the masculinity in Ciaran brought the beast out of her and made every fiber of her being vibrate.

He quickly led Madeline through layers of doors. The place was like a maze. Ciaran opened a steel door, revealing a room that looked like an enormous security scanner. "Leave any electronic equipment out here, including your camera or recorder. This scanner will wipe and destroy everything and anything that has a memory capability."

"Thanks. Good to know. I can't afford to lose this." Madeline took her camera and recorder out. "They're my life, you know!"

Ciaran smiled. "I wager."

He led Madeline through the scanner and into the control room. Madeline had never seen anything like it. The room was packed with endless rows of computer mainframes and monitors. She didn't know what the ten people in the room were doing, but they stopped and greeted Ciaran as he walked in. Ciaran responded with a friendly but authoritative nod. Whatever they were doing, she was sure it wasn't medicine they were making.

"This is just the electronic security control of the head-quarters," Ciaran explained. "We don't make medicine here. Would you like a tour of the labs?" Ciaran gestured toward a series of monitors which displayed multiple screens of pharmaceutical labs, where several people in white coats were working.

"They're working at this hour?"

Ciaran chuckled. "Yes, at this hour, precisely, but not London time. These are the Australian labs you're looking at. It's office hours over there. They focus on the Asian-

Pacific range. These are the London labs, here, in this head-quarters." Ciaran pointed toward a couple of screens in the corner. "We develop new and important products here. Our overseas labs are mainly for production, not development."

Madeline nodded. "I appreciate you showing me all this. The security and the operation are very impressive."

"We operate within legal boundaries. We have strict security to protect us against the competition. Also to protect the consumer from any imperfect practice. We are responsible for what we do. Nothing comes in or goes out without scanning and quarantine. We are not media friendly, as you have mentioned, but we have nothing to hide. We just protect our privacy."

Madeline gave Ciaran a moment after his eloquent speech. "You must be proud of your family."

"You can meet them, if you like. They don't bite." Ciaran smiled.

Befriend the LeBlancs? Not in this lifetime. She wasn't cut out for this social circus. She never forgot where she came from.

"Could we look at the computer usage, please? I don't want to know more than I need to."

"As you like." Ciaran smiled politely and gestured toward a small door.

They entered a smaller room. Ciaran rolled up his sleeves and manually operated the mainframe computer. Madeline looked at him. *What a scene!* She could not believe that he manned the computer himself like this. She thought he would summon one of his technicians to ask for a report.

Codes and commands flowed through the monitor, none of which she knew or even recognized.

A river of paper streamed out from a printer. Ciaran

fetched the paper and brought it toward Madeline. He tore off the last couple of pages.

"This is the summary of the computer usage in all of our international headquarters." He gestured toward the river of paper. "I can't give you the detailed log, but you can have this report." He pointed to a table. "As you can see, no computer in any of our headquarters was used for interactive game play in the last three months. Specifically, working computers have supremely advanced firewalls. No foreign programs could be installed. No one would be able to play any games from our headquarters, Madeline."

Madeline shook her head.

"I can extend the search window to six months if you like, but I doubt it would make a difference, as the incident with your friend's game sounded recent."

A pounding headache ripped through her head.

"I can't ban employees from game play during working hours. But as you have seen, no foreign electronic objects with any game-playing capacity can pass through the scanner. There's no reason—and no way—for an employee to smuggle a computer into the workplace just to play games."

"Are you sure?" Her brain had stopped working. *A dead end!* She thought.

"This is the bloodline of our entire organization. When it comes to security, yes, I am very sure about it. Whatever your friend is looking for, it's not here, Madeline."

He led her out of the room.

After they had gone back through the scanner, Madeline put her camera and recorder into her bag.

She felt the warmth of his hand when he lifted her chin up. "Are you okay?" Those intense gray eyes looked at her with genuine concern.

She nodded. "Oh God, oh no, my phone . . ." Madeline

pulled out her prepaid phone from her pocket. She had totally forgotten about it and had taken it through the scanner.

"Don't worry, it happens all the time," he said quickly and opened a small cabinet containing lots of cell phones. He picked one up, activated it, and gave it to Madeline. "Take this. It's prepaid. You can throw it away when you no longer need it. You'll have to reload your address book. You can log in online to change your username and password and put more credit in if you want to use it longer. At the moment, the password is your name. The credit is enough for normal usage for about a week if you call internationally, and a month for domestic calls."

He was staring at her face again and she was doing her best to hold back her tears.

"Oh, for pity's sake, can you tell me what's going on? What is the bloody game? What exactly is your friend looking for?"

"Could you please take me home?" Madeline murmured weakly. She hated the sound of her voice at the moment. She just didn't know what to do next. She needed time to think. There was nothing Ciaran could do to help. Right now, she needed her space.

Ciaran said something else to her, but she couldn't register the information.

In front of her apartment, Ciaran kissed Madeline good night. "I guess I should say good morning. It's two a.m."

"Oh . . . I'm sorry. I shouldn't have kept you that long. Thanks for all your help."

"This is my direct number. I'll be in France for a couple of days, in and out of meetings. I'd appreciate it if you'd be discreet regarding to my whereabouts. But please call if you need anything."

She looked at him. The magnificent Ciaran LeBlanc

from the most mysterious— and possibly the richest—family on the planet was giving her his phone number just like any guy looking for a second date.

And she had used him this evening. She'd just given him a load of big fat lies. She wouldn't even do that to a pseudo-acquaintance.

Tomorrow, she would be watching her friend die because she could not get the lousy names of some computer-game fanatics. Yet she was proud of herself for being a good journalist. This had to be fate's biggest joke on her yet.

"Is there anything you want to tell me? Anything that I can help with?"

She couldn't get a word past her lips. She seriously need her space right now, and she needed to crash.

"You're tired. Get some sleep," Ciaran said in response to Madeline's silence.

Madeline nodded slightly. "Thanks. Bye, Ciaran." As cliché as it sounded, that was all she could say.

CHAPTER 11

*T*he next morning, as expected, Zen called. Madeline let the phone ring ten times before she picked up.

"What's with the new phone number?" Zen asked.

"Dropped and broke the other one. Put the video on—I want to see Jo."

Zen obliged, tilting the phone so that Madeline could see her friend. She was so pale and still drugged. But she knew that the second Jo was able to get free of her shackles, Zen wouldn't stand a chance.

"I expect some good news, Maddie," Zen threatened.

Madeline grabbed her cup of coffee, glancing at a painting on the wall of her apartment. After a sip of coffee, she spoke calmly into the phone.

"Samuel Kandinsky, that's the name."

Zen's eyes widened.

Jo stared at Madeline. Even with all the physical restraints and the effects of the sedative, the half-conscious Jo knew that Madeline had lied. She looked at Madeline, questioning her with her eyes, but said nothing.

"Give me contact details so I can talk to him."

"That wasn't the deal, Zen. The name is all I've got. Getting that name out of the LeBlanc headquarters was hard enough. I have seen the guy, so I can draw him out as we agreed. But he didn't exactly hand me his CV and contact details."

"You were inside the LeBlanc headquarters?"

"Impressive, huh? I spoke to Ciaran LeBlanc myself. I'm sure Samuel is your dude. He's probably off work by now. Do you want me to talk to him, or do you want to do it yourself?"

"No, no, I'll do that myself." Zen's eyes sparked with anticipation.

"When will you let Jo go? You want to talk to the guy yourself, so as far as I'm concerned, my task is finished."

"No, no, there's a step two. We talked about this."

Madeline clenched her teeth. "The last one?"

"Yes, and this one's easy. There is an alchemist named John Dee. He died in the 1500s and is buried in Mortlake. You go there and get me an artifact that was buried with him. It's only an hour or so outside of London. Piece of cake. The guy died a long time ago. Nobody will pay any attention to what you're doing."

Madeline stared at Zen for a long moment and raised an eyebrow. "Say that again?"

Zen exhaled to calm himself. "John Dee was . . ."

"I heard that part—you don't have to repeat it. You really want me to dig up the grave of some dead alchemist?"

"Well, it's not exactly tomb raider. All you need is a shovel."

"Why don't you do it yourself?"

"I could, but it wouldn't be very efficient. I'll have to get Jo to London to negotiate with White Knight. Then once he agrees, the artifact has to be available for him to work on. I can't be in two places at the same time!"

"Alchemists are those who squeezed gold out of steel, right? If you're after gold, wouldn't it be easier just to rob banks or jewelry stores?"

"Just like most ordinary people, you're very short-sighted, Maddie. Get me the artifact, then we'll talk. I might even give you some gold dust if you cooperate!"

Madeline rolled her eye exaggeratedly so that Zen could see it. "Yeah, right. So what's the 'artifact'? And when will you need it?"

"You'll know it when you see it. I don't know exactly what it is. It had to have been something of great importance to John Dee. I'll need it within twenty-four hours."

"You've—"

"No, I'm not kidding. I'll get the plane tickets now. We'll be there in twenty-four hours. I need you to have the artifact ready and locate the White Knight for me." He paused and stared at Madeline. "The timing here is very critical. If you mess me up, I'll have no mercy for you and your little friend here."

Madeline stared back at him sternly. "Jo can't travel long distances without her meds. If you paid any attention at all and stopped drugging her, she'd tell you that she's diabetic and is probably overdue for her doses right now."

Zen scratched his head in frustration. Madeline could hear him cursing to himself. "All right, I'll get her the meds she needs. Do you know where she gets them?"

"Ask her yourself. If I remember correctly, it's somewhere in Midtown—between Park and Madison."

Zen nodded and noted it down.

Madeline smiled. "I can dig up an old grave. I'm sure the dead people won't mind. And I can get one ready for you, too—and bury you with pleasure."

Zen grinned crookedly. "See you soon," he said and hung up abruptly.

As soon as the screen went black, a tear trickled down Madeline's face. She quickly brushed it away and found her hand shaking. She couldn't afford to be shaky right now. She needed to focus.

She had flirted with fire.

CHAPTER 12

*M*adeline took a deep breath. She gazed at the phone for short moment and quickly sketched a plan in her head.

Then she dialed. At the other end, Stephen's sleepy voice came across the line.

"You're sleeping at this hour, Stephen?"

"Madeline? Where've you been? I stopped by your office, and Paul said you're on vacation! You? Taking a vacation? Sounded almost as unlikely as breaking news of an alien invasion."

"I'm in London."

"Wow. You're really on a vacation."

"Listen, I need your help."

"Sure."

Madeline pulled hard at her ponytail as a form of self-punishment. "Really, Stephen? You don't even need to know what I'm asking you to do?"

"No, really. Okay, yes, so tell me what you want me to do."

"You know Zen, Jo's boss, right?"

"Yes, I saw him once at Jo's office. What about him?"

"This is going to sound weird, but it's serious, so please bear with me. Zen kidnapped Jo because of some role-playing interactive game Jo developed. He wanted me to come to London to find the guy who played a character in Jo's game. Zen beat Jo, and he's threatened to rape her if I can't find this guy."

There was a long pause. "And you didn't think calling the cops should be your first course of action?"

"How fast do you think the cops can pull their acts together in this case? Zen didn't ask for money or anything that the cops can leverage on. He wanted me to get information about a computer geek. Getting information is what I do for a living, Stephen. He sent me Jo's necklace and said if I make one wrong move, he'll kill Jo."

"And you didn't even think of calling me? Not as a cop, but as a friend?"

Madeline had never heard Stephen raise his voice before. They had been friends for more than five years. He'd asked Madeline out once, and she hadn't budged, so they'd settled on being friends. There were countless times Madeline had asked herself why she'd rejected Stephen and couldn't find a good answer.

"Stephen, I'm telling you now."

"I'll have him in jail within an hour."

"Be careful, Stephen. He came close to raping Jo yesterday. He's going crazy. He'd cut her throat if I said one wrong thing. I gave him what he wanted to hear. I told him I got the guy, and now Zen's on his way to London."

Another long pause from Stephen's end. "You don't sound like you've got the guy."

"No, I don't."

"Right. . . Okay, I'll find an excuse to detain him, legally or not. How does that sound?"

"Uhhhmm . . ."

"I'll beat the shit out of him and get Jo back then. How does that sound?

"Be careful, Stephen. I don't want you to get hurt."

Stephen snorted.

"Zen would have made up an excuse to Jo's family about her disappearance. She took off to write her games all the time. He wouldn't be stupid enough to hide her at his place. I tricked him by saying that Jo needed diabetic meds. She was half unconscious, but I think she understood. If she can fool him, he'll be at a drugstore in Manhattan for the medicine."

Stephen said irritably, "I'm a cop, Madeline. I can track this guy down, all right? Plus, Zen's record isn't exactly spotless. I ran him once. But I can get Jo out, okay? Don't you worry."

Madeline felt a wave of relief. "I should have called you earlier."

"You're telling me now. That's good enough."

Madeline closed her eyes and still couldn't figure out why she hadn't given Stephen a chance before. Then she saw the blue dots hovering in the corner of her room. "You've got to be kidding me," she muttered.

"Huh?"

"No, not you. I've got to go now, Stephen. Would you call me back and let me know what happens?"

"I'll call you when I've got Zen."

Madeline hung up the phone.

She slowly approached the dots. They swiveled, did a little dance, and grew to the size of soccer balls. She had never seen them this close before—so close she could feel the vibration they emitted. She reached her hand out to touch them. The closer her hand came to them, the stronger the suction felt. It intensified until she felt nothing but an explosion of blue.

CHAPTER 13

*C*iaran glanced around the boardroom at the twelve directors sitting at the long shiny table. While they were busy taking notes on what he just said, Ciaran scanned the agenda in front of him. He frowned at the last two items and looked up.

"It's too premature to discuss the last two points on this agenda. That means the meeting today is concluded. Any questions?"

There was a murmuring in the room, brief discussions here and there, and then everyone seemed to be eager to move on with the day. Ciaran dismissed the meeting. As soon as the last person left, he turned on the video call. An image of a man in his sixties flashed on the screen.

"Doctor Thomas, how's Mother?" Ciaran asked.

Doctor Thomas smiled. "Ciaran, your mother is fine. It was just a mild flu. She is as stubborn as you are. Didn't want to take any medicine. . ."

Ciaran raised an eyebrow, and the corner of his mouth quirked waiting for Doctor Thomas to finish.

". . . She loves her organic vegetable garden and refuses

to eat anything that's not from there. She's never questioned how those vegetables survive in the Dublin weather. You've done a good job, Ciaran."

Ciaran smiled. "Thanks for looking after my mother, Doctor Thomas. I don't know what I'd do without you."

"Don't exaggerate, Ciaran. You always know what to do. Are you well?"

"Yes. Why do you ask?"

Doctor Thomas sighed. "I was there when your mother introduced you to this world. You don't think I'd know how you look when you're well?"

Ciaran laughed. He liked Doctor Thomas's gentle voice, especially when he tried to put on that authoritative tone. Most of the time, it didn't work for Ciaran, but he loved to hear it anyway. Ciaran realized that he was squeezing the pen in his hand a bit too hard, and he put it down on a pile of papers. A long, long time ago, he would hear that same authoritative voice from his father, and it always worked on him.

Ciaran ignored his pounding migraine and smiled. "I'm fine. Really."

Doctor Thomas nodded. "Fine. Go take the painkillers. I'm sure they'll fix it. Would you like me to send your regards to your mother?"

Ciaran stared at the screen. Doctor Thomas sighed again. "I guess not. Goodbye for now, son." He smiled and turned off the call.

Ciaran grabbed the desk phone, and when his assistant's voice came across, he said, "Could you cancel my meeting this afternoon, please? I'll get Lily in the London office to notify you with the reschedule." He then grabbed his jacket and his coat, and headed out of the room.

~

HALF AN HOUR LATER, Ciaran stood in front of a dusty steel door. He stared at it for a long moment, then punched in a code.

The door whined and squeaked as it opened. The lab light automatically lit up, and the musty air greeted him. Ciaran threw this coat on a steel bench.

He entered a security code on a keypad beside a cabinet and opened it. Inside was a row of medicines in colorful jars. He took a small tube from the end of the row and placed it on the bench. He stared at the tube for a long moment as it glared back at him in challenge.

The migraine had come back in the last two weeks, and it was unbearable. It was pounding in his head right now.

A soothing female voice echoed in his head, "I made this for you. Why put up with the pain, Ciaran? Just take it."

His vision blurred with the pain, his body swayed, and he braced his hands on the bench top to keep his balance.

"You don't know how much pain I can endure. I deserve this," he muttered to himself.

He grunted as the pain intensified. Beads of sweat began to trickle slowly down his forehead. The sharp pain pierced through his brain and before he knew it, he passed out on the cold dusty floor.

CHAPTER 14

*M*adeline scrambled up from the floor, the sensation of the blue suction still pounding in her head. "What the hell?" she muttered. Then she recalled the vision. "Okay, stupid blue dots," she muttered, "Guide me if you're any good."

An hour later, she followed the blue dots into the British museum where a gold plate that had once used by John Dee to communicate to spirits stared at her from a display cabinet. Madeline shook her head and rolled her eyes. Based on her research, John Dee had been an astrologist and advisor to Queen Elizabeth I. In some capacity, he was an alchemist, but it didn't seem as if alchemy was how he had gained fame.

She muttered to herself, "If you knew how to make gold, you wouldn't have died poor."

Her research suggested that John Dee had died in poverty. He couldn't possibly have made—or had known how to make—gold.

The blue dots disappeared. "Right, just reappear whenever you feel like it." Madeline cursed in frustration and noticed that the people standing next to her turned to look. She shrugged and scurried outside the museum.

She wasn't out of the woods yet—not until Stephen let her know he had gotten Zen, and Jo was safe. Just in case Zen turned up, she had to come up with some artifact. She figured she'd better go digging now. She shook her head, not sure what to feel. Next, she had to do something about the *fictional* character Samuel, who played the *fictional* character White Knight in some *fictional* computer game Jo had created!

Madeline hired a car and headed out of London. Hearing the shovel rattling in the trunk of the car, she shook her head in disbelief about what she was about to do.

The blue dots were no longer directing her, so she was going to have to rely on technology. The portable GPS, called Tom, that she had requested with the car was blurting out the instructions in a monotone female voice. She had to remember to drive on the left-hand side of the road. After a couple of wrong turns, she started to scold the machine, "You're female, why in world do they call you Tom? Is that why you don't understand that I have to not only get from A to B in one piece but also have to drive on the opposite side of the road?"

The machine didn't answer her.

While trying to dodge a black cab that was honking at her, Madeline heard the machine instruct, "In 200 yards, turn left."

"So much for English manners," Madeline muttered to herself, thinking of the black cab.

She glanced ahead and gestured to the machine. "Turn left into what?" Then she realized that she was talking to the machine again, and of course, there would not be a response. Madeline made a guess and turned left onto a smaller, paved road, only to discover that it was a dead end.

The machine calmly instructed, "Make a U-turn when possible."

"Of course," Madeline spoke to herself.

She turned into a private driveway and made a U-turn. She heard a dog barking at her from inside a peaceful cottage at the end of the driveway.

"Bark away, and bark real loud, 'cause you can't bite me!"

Madeline turned left on the next block and was relieved because there was no objection from Tom-the-guide.

"You have arrived at your destination," the machine cheerfully announced.

Madeline stared at the destination—it was a roundabout.

She didn't want to waste any more time arguing with the machine, so she parked on a small street and walked toward St Mary's Church.

It was a beautiful church. Based on Madeline's research this morning, this was where she might find some useful information. She stood at the entrance of the church, staring at the door as if admiring its magnificence. Instead, a stream of strategies flew through her head, none of them viable.

Going inside and asking for the grave of John Dee so that she could dig it up wouldn't go down well. The church did publicize that they had no information about the exact location of the tomb. Of course they had to say that they did not know where the tomb was, Madeline deduced. It would only take a few more scumbags like Zen, and the church would have a gold rush on its hands.

The door of the church slid open and a lady in a beige

sweater and a light green coat walked out. Noticing Madeline, she approached. "May I help you?"

"Ah, my name is Madeline Roux. I'm working on a research project on theology. I'd like to see Doctor John Dee's plaque and some exhibits of his life and his work, if possible, but I notice that you don't have a service today and aren't open to public visits."

"Oh, I'm Maggie. I don't work here. I'm visiting my friends. But you've come to the right place for this. They've just obtained some funds from the government, along with generous public donations, to make the plaque. They've organized an association in the name of Doctor John Dee of Mortlake. Let me tell you, they're very proud of it. Or I should say, we are so proud of the doctor for his achievements. We appreciate the recognition he brought to Mortlake. Even Queen Elizabeth visited his house. Come on in." Maggie churned out a stream of information that Madeline had known from her research. But she politely followed Maggie inside the church.

"Waste of time!" said an old man sitting on the steps in front of the church.

"Excuse me?" Madeline stepped back outside.

Maggie interrupted. "Oh, Shaun, aren't you supposed to be at the library? Don't tell me you're drunk again at this hour?"

There were some movements from beneath a thick carpet of beard on Shaun's face. Madeline suspected it was a grin to Lady Maggie.

"It's winter, Maggie. There isn't much to do in the gardens. People go to a public library to read, not to look at flowers in the gardens. I'm waiting for you here, my lady! You're my flower." Shaun stood up and approached Maggie.

"Excuse me, I'm sorry to interrupt. You were saying

something about me wasting time?" Aware of her time constraints, Madeline butted in.

"Ah, at least three times in the last month I saw people asking the same questions as you did, looking at the doctor's stuff as if they admired him. Then they ended up searching the graveyard for his tomb. Let me tell you now, it's a waste of time."

Maggie looked astonished. "Shaun, have you been stalking the church?"

"Oh no, I would never do such a thing!"

Feeling uneasy, Madeline shifted her shoulders. "What's wrong if people just want to show their respect at his tomb?"

Shaun laughed. "I don't think they wanted to show respect. They looked like they wanted to dig out the gold he buried with him!"

"Don't say such a thing, Shaun. It's not nice, and it's disrespectful to the doctor," Maggie protested.

Shaun looked at Madeline. "You see, now I've upset my lady. Look, I don't care if you want the gold in his coffin or not—he wasn't buried here."

"How do you know that?" Maggie's voice was high-pitched.

Shaun smiled secretly. "A man knows many secrets!"

Maggie put her hands on her hips, insistent.

"All right, all right. I helped Mrs. Hanson with her gardens many times. That's what I got as payment—stories. You know her. Full of mysterious stories."

"Mrs. Hanson in the Rose cottage?"

"Green Rose's cottage."

"There is no such thing as a green rose."

Madeline raised her hands apologetically as if she was intruding on their conversation once again. "I'm sorry. I've got to go. As I said, I just wanted to show some respect at the tomb. But if it's not here, then there's no point in me wasting your time. I'll make a donation to the church."

"Oh no, you should come in for a cup of tea," Maggie chirped.

"If you want the gold, talk to Mrs. Hanson. She knows the secrets! Her cottage is just at the next block." Shaun winked at Madeline. Then he turned to Maggie. "You see, I'm a good man. I don't have greed in me. I'm not digging graves for gold."

Madeline's phone rang. She grabbed at it like a drowning person grabbing at a life preserver and went to a quiet corner to talk.

At the other end of the line, Stephen's voice sounded scratchy. Madeline noted that it was the middle of the night in New York. "I'm sorry, Madeline!"

Madeline felt a chill run down her spine. Instead of asking nonsense questions, she waited.

"I messed everything up," Stephen continued. "I ran some information on Zen after I talked to you. I found out he owns a cabin in the hunting ground in the national park. I couldn't help it . . . I went there. It was in the middle of the night, you know, and I figured if he'd hidden Jo there, then I could wrap it up sweet."

"Bottom line, Stephen, is Jo okay?"

"Yeah. She is. She's valuable to Zen. He'd pull the trigger on me, not on her."

"What? A gunfight? He shot at you? Are you okay?"

"Just a scratch. I'm fine. But it was unfair to have five of them on one of me, and I couldn't fire the weapon without reciting the procedures—I wasn't there in an official capacity."

Madeline sat down on a bench.

Stephen continued, "He recognized me as Jo's friend. He knew I was a cop."

"But he still shot at you?"

"If I'd been in my official position, he wouldn't—"

"I know, Stephen. I understand, and I'm sorry I put you in danger."

"Danger is a package deal with my job. I can't believe a computer geek like Zen would run a full-on organized crime hub in the middle of a jungle. They were all armed."

Madeline muttered, "He wants a lot more than just winning a computer game."

"What do you mean?"

"Oh, nothing. So he knew I sent you, and now he's coming after me?"

"There wasn't any time to talk or ask any questions. All shooting and shouting. He fled, taking Jo with him. It sounded like he was heading straight to the airport. Even if I'd pulled in my buddies, it would—"

"I understand. You don't know which flight, which route, how long it would take him to get to me?"

"I'm coming over there, Madeline."

"No, please don't. I can take care of myself. I've asked enough of you."

Stephen lowered his voice, "And I'm not asking anything of you. I just want to you count on me. Just this time. Trust me. Let me help you."

"Stephen!"

"I'll get Zen, and I'll find you, Madeline."

Stephen hung up the phone. It was the first time Stephen had hung up on her. Most of the time, she was the one cutting off a conversation.

CHAPTER 15

*C*iaran stopped and waited patiently. A couple more blocks to his London headquarters, and the traffic had been crawling for fifteen minutes. Lindsay called again, and Ciaran picked up on his car phone. "You go ahead with your meetings, Lindsay. I'm not scheduled to be in the office, so you don't have to wait for me there."

"Are you sure? Robert wants to talk to you beforehand, and he said you didn't pick up."

That must have been when he passed out, Ciaran thought. "Ask him to wait for me in the office. I'll be there as soon as this mess clears up."

"What happened?"

"Traffic jam, I think. A couple of blocks from our south gate."

Ciaran inched the car ahead as the traffic controller signaled.

"Do you want to leave the car there? I'll send someone to pick you up, going the other way to the north gate."

"It's okay. I'm nearly there. Don't worry. I'll see you soon." Ciaran hung up as the police signaled him to move forward, and he made significant progress. Ciaran drove ahead. It was actually good timing. He needed this time to settle his headache. He still felt a bit shaky from the effects of it. It had been bad before, but never that nasty. What he needed right now was a strong dose of painkillers.

An officer tapped on the windshield to signal Ciaran to move ahead. He pressed the button to lower the window. "What's happening, officer?"

"A homeless person died."

"Accident?"

"I don't know. He just lay there and died on the sidewalk. They've nearly cleaned up the scene. It won't take long."

"Thank you."

This was going to take forever, Ciaran thought. He reached his hand out toward the control panel to take Lindsay up on his offer, but before he dialed, he saw a puppy standing right in front of his car. If he had inched the car ahead without looking, he would have run over the dog.

It wasn't just any puppy—it was a small, shabby Alaskan malamute pup wearing a dark saddle and a sign around its neck saying, "I've lost my mommy, and I need to eat." It was obvious that this dog had belonged to the homeless person, whoever that might have been. Ciaran glanced to the side window, looking for the officer he'd just spoken to, but he didn't see him. He glanced in his rear view mirror and saw a line of cars.

The puppy shivered. Its eyes were teary, and its fur soaked with the moisture from the winter air. Ciaran looked for the officer again and found no one. The car in front of him had moved up. He cursed and sneaked open the passenger door. The puppy didn't wait for an invitation

—he jumped right in. Ciaran drove the car forward and waited in the traffic again.

"Let me take that sign off your neck. It annoys the heck out of me." He pulled off the sign and could feel the puppy shaking. Ciaran cranked up the heat, and warm air pumped out of the floor unit. The puppy dove right in front of the heater and rubbed against it, rolling on the floor as if in ecstasy. When its fur dried out, it sat up straight on the floor, looking at Ciaran. Then it raised a front leg in a handshake position.

Ciaran laughed. "You're very welcome, smart dog. I'm sure he taught you how to pick pockets, too. That's a pity. I don't do dogs, let alone a puppy." Ciaran's car had crawled up alongside the sidewalk where the homeless person had died. The body had been taken away, but a pile of rags and a crooked shopping trolley full of junk were still on the sidewalk. Next to the trolley was a small carton wrapped with rags that Ciaran was sure the person had used as the dog's bed.

Some officers were still standing around clearing the scene. "There you go. No need to thank me for the ride," Ciaran said and opened the passenger door. The puppy tried its last trick, looking at Ciaran with watery eyes. He shook his head and gestured toward the door. The puppy looked down to the floor, grabbed the sign Ciaran had peeled off its neck, and jumped out of the car.

Ciaran glanced in the rear view mirror and saw the puppy sitting on the road, watching with the sign in its mouth. He drove a bit more and stopped again for traffic. The puppy still sat there. Then an officer approached, and the puppy stood up and withdrew from the officer's reach. By doing so, he stepped backward out to the road. Another officer approached to help, and the dog backed further out onto the road.

The traffic was finally clear, and cars started moving fast. Ciaran cursed. He reached over and opened the passenger door again. From the rear mirror, he could see the puppy racing toward his car. In seconds, it stood at the door.

"I don't like that sign," Ciaran said.

In a heartbeat, the dog dropped the sign onto the road and hopped into the car.

CHAPTER 16

*T*his was a total screw-up, Madeline thought. Stephen not only couldn't get Zen, but had alerted him that she had sent a cop in. Now she had to execute the plan B she didn't even have.

She had to find someone to play the Samuel she had created. That was her priority. But she had to find the artifact first. That was a priority, too. She could explain to Zen somehow that it had taken more time to find the artifact, but she could not make an excuse for not providing Samuel. Maybe she should find the artifact, and then come clean to Zen about Samuel, using the artifact to compensate him? No, that wouldn't work.

She was in Mortlake anyway, so she would see what she could do. If Zen couldn't speak to her directly, he couldn't jump to any conclusions about anything too soon. As long as he was unsure, Jo would be fine, Madeline contemplated.

Madeline drove around the block to the Green Rose cottage and approached the small gate on foot. The black

Pomeranian who had been barking at Madeline that morning was now baring his teeth at her. *Not very friendly*, she thought and gave the dog a stern look.

A woman in her nineties—or at least looked that old—dressed in gypsy clothes appeared at the doorstep.

"I've convinced Woody to forgive your intrusion this morning, but he's still upset, you see!"

"Mrs. Hanson, I'm so sorry I was rude this morning, but I . . ."

"All your kind are the same. So don't even mention it."

"My kind? Mrs. Hanson . . ." Madeline raised her voice in defense, but Mrs. Hanson cut in.

"You want to find John Dee's grave, right?" Mrs. Hanson smiled.

"Yes, I do. But I wasn't . . ."

Mrs. Hanson raised a hand to cut Madeline off.

"What you want to find in the grave is not my problem. I knew you were coming. You're just like the others. Greed will not bring anyone any good."

"But I didn't . . ."

"You do not have greed in you. I can see that. But you have grief. The grief you are carrying is horrible—and it's contagious. So stay far from me. Greed is easy for me to handle. I can help with that. But you will have to sort out the grief yourself."

She had no idea what the old lady was prattling on about. But something weighed heavily in her chest. It hurt. But there was no time to think about it. She had a task at hand, and her friend's life depended on it.

"Where can I find the grave?"

"Fosse Way. It's guarded by Roman soldiers. But I have to warn you, young lady, these soldiers cannot tell the difference between greed and grief. They will judge you by your actions. So be careful."

Mrs. Hanson turned around and disappeared suddenly behind the door. Madeline looked down to the dog and found that it, too, had gone.

She walked away from the manicured garden.

Right, so plan C then.

CHAPTER 17

Fatigue dragged at Madeline. The fact the she'd only slept a couple of hours a day in the last week was one factor in her exhaustion, but hunger was gnawing at her as well.

She got into her car and programmed the GPS for Fosse Way. The machine couldn't locate it. *Was it a road, a district, or a city?* Madeline just wanted to see how far it was from her current location.

She didn't have her laptop with her, so she used the phone Ciaran gave her instead. It was a smart phone with some data capability for temporarily usage. Ciaran wouldn't settle for anything less, of course. Madeline smiled to herself, remembering the look on his face when he had programmed her phone.

Google maps suggested that Fosse Way was a highway which connected several different towns and ran for more than 350 km. There were smaller sections of the road that deviated from the main road, and part of it was called Roman Road. That had to be it. She didn't have much time to research, but Mrs. Hanson had mentioned Roman soldiers. That narrowed things down a lot for her.

She tapped her fingers on the steering wheel. "Just a quick search, and I'll be back in London in no time," she muttered to herself. At least if she had to encounter Zen sometime tomorrow, she would have something to show him so she could stall for more time.

As the GPS had become useless at this point, Madeline used Google Maps and hit the road. By her gauge, it would take a couple of hours to get to Roman Road.

"I could use a blue dot right about now," she said out loud. Nothing. She shook her head. She'd thought the psychic dots weren't random, but they were really playing tricks on her.

After a couple of hours, she could see signs pointing to her destination. She veered off the highway, bearing in mind that she could come back to it at any time.

The smaller roads were a bit bumpy, but she figured as long as there were signs of civilization, she would be fine. It was going to be getting dark, so she knew she'd better find Roman Road soon, wherever it was. She was about to give up and turn around when she finally saw it—a small, narrow country road with stone walls running along it.

Wow. That was the only word Madeline could think of. The walls must have been more than a thousand years old. They were only knee-high, a meter at most. But they went on and on, black stones stacked together, forming what seemed to be the walls of time. If they could talk, Madeline bet they could tell stories. They had witnessed the history of a thousand years or more. Many people had lived and died here. Behind the stone walls were endless green fields, ditches, and marshes. Madeline was amazed. She was just a few hours outside vibrant London—and this!

The walls were mysterious, but there was no sign of a

graveyard or even a single tomb. She didn't see how John Dee could be buried here.

The air seemed to have grown thicker, and the wind had stopped blowing. It was eerily quiet. Something kept urging her to go ahead. An ancient voice. A haunting chant.

Something was watching her.

Urging

Pushing.

Clouding her judgment.

It turned dark quickly. She wanted to turn around, but she couldn't seem to sync her mind and her actions. It wasn't possible to turn the car around on this narrow one-lane road. It was so narrow that two cars couldn't pass at the same time.

Madeline checked Google Maps to see how close she was to the main road and discovered the phone was totally dead—the battery was drained.

No worries, she thought as she turned on her GPS and programmed in her address in London as the destination. The machine flashed once, twice, and then it went blank.

Madeline glanced out the windows. It was completely dark now. The chanting still hovered in the air, and the wind started to weave through the stones and trees, making eerie flute-like sounds. She needed her blue dots, but she knew very well from experience that they wouldn't come to her when she needed them most.

She had to turn the car around somehow.

Madeline saw a broken part of the wall and veered toward it. In the beam of the car headlights, it appeared to be a grass field on the other side of the wall, not a swamp or a river. She was close to the gap in the wall when the car was suddenly pushed forward. A loud bang echoed in the interior of the car when it hit the stone wall, making her head ring. Still having momentum, she managed to steer back to the road, scraping the side of the car along the stone wall. It sloped down a bit. Maybe it was her imagination, but the car seemed to keep speeding forward. She hit the brakes.

It didn't work.

She kept hitting loose stones and tree logs, and the car swung from one side to another, but it kept moving forward.

For a very brief moment, Madeline thought she saw a line of Roman soldiers marching along the wall. She shook her head. She knew fatigue was dragging at her now. Her head seemed to weigh a ton, and her mind was drifting, unfocused.

She hit the brakes again. It didn't work.

She saw the Roman soldiers once more. One soldier turned around and looked straight at her. His eyes were evil and red. She pressed the accelerator.

It worked.

As she zoomed past, the soldier raised his body-length sword and his metal shield and threw his weight at the side of the car.

The car hit another log, jumped in the air, and almost flipped over.

Madeline drove faster. She didn't realize that she was crying. Her headlights shone on armory, weapons, and marching soldiers.

There was lightning sparking from the sky and flashing on the road right in front of her car. Madeline veered off the road.

But then she saw her blue dot. And another one. Many of them, flying over the sky in a flock. But it was too late now. The car flew over a wall, landing on a slope and rolling until it hit a large rock and lay motionless.

Am I dead? She couldn't move for long time as she was pinned between the seat and the airbag.

Then she heard footsteps. Madeline kicked hard and wriggled to free herself. She stumbled out of the car and looked up to the top of the ditch. Lightning cast light into the darkness of stone and trees. She saw the soldiers and their shadows. She heard them murmur in their search for her.

Which way is London? She scanned the vicinity aimlessly. The lightning created a spotlight right where she was standing. Thunder roamed across the sky. Madeline yelped and jumped aside to hide.

Too late. They had seen her.

The shadows moved toward her. They called her name. She ran. They chased. She kept running.

Madeline fell, rolling on rocks and tree branches. She scrambled up and kept moving.

She heard her name again. But this time, the voice sounded familiar. She knew that voice.

Lightning again, and in the brightness of the flashing light, she saw Ciaran running toward her. It was him. She couldn't be mistaken. She recognized the shape of him, and the sound of his voice.

"Madeline!" Ciaran shouted.

He rushed forward and grabbed her to stop her from running. They both tumbled and rolled on the hard rocks.

Ciaran helped her up. Madeline grabbed on to him. She felt like weeping. In fact, she *was*. Ciaran held her tight for a very brief second and pushed her to continue running.

Madeline was dazed. "Why are we running? You're here. We're safe."

Ciaran pulled at her. "Run!" he said.

Madeline didn't quite get it, but she went with him.

Lightning, thunder, and now pouring rain made it

impossible to tell what they were running toward. Madeline guessed he was trying to get her to run toward the light. It felt right, running to the light.

She still heard footsteps and saw shadows. It was not clear to her who they were running toward and who they were running from.

A barrage of large stones flew toward them.

It had to be from the Roman soldiers, Madeline thought. She could see the holes the stones made in the mud, the walls, and tree trunks around them.

Ciaran grabbed Madeline and pushed her down to avoid the raining stones. He was covering her, Madeline knew.

And then silence, as if the sound had been suddenly vacuumed out of the sphere.

They stood up. She heard a whooshing noise, and then the stones commenced again. Both Ciaran and Madeline fell, rolling down a slope. Then she felt cold water. They might be in a pool, a pond, a lake—but it was cold.

That was the last thing she remembered before the world went black.

CHAPTER 18

Thick embroidered curtains dripping with ropes and ribbons in royal colors hung around the bed and from the ceiling, looking down at Madeline.

Have I time-traveled? Madeline blinked and glanced around.

She was lying on a four-poster bed in the middle of a spacious room surrounded by walls covered in deep-colored patterned wallpaper and tapestries. Paintings in fancy frames were arranged on the walls at every corner of the room. Even the bedside lamps were ornate.

Had it not been for the sight of Ciaran standing at the window in his modern clothing, talking on his cell phone, Madeline would have argued that this was a castle straight out of the fifteenth century.

Ciaran murmured something in French. The language sounded like music to Madeline. Then, sensing Madeline's gaze, he finished the conversation and turned around.

He completes the scene, Madeline thought. Complementing the setting of the room, he looked like a king. His long hair was swept back, revealing a broad forehead and sculptured face—the face of a dark angel. He was too young to be a king, but she couldn't settle for a lesser description.

Within seconds, as quick and gentle as a cat, he was at her bedside.

"How are you feeling?" Ciaran slid the phone into his pocket.

Madeline moved her shoulders a bit. She ached everywhere. "I've been better . . . Are we in a castle? Is this your house?"

Ciaran grinned. "Yes, we are indeed in a castle. But this is not my house. It's Lumley Castle, converted into a hotel. It's the closest place I could find where the helicopter could drop us as you didn't want to go to the hospital, nor did you want me to contact the authorities regarding the incident last night. So the Queen Suite is what you have here."

"The haunted Lumley Castle?" Madeline's eyes widened.

Ciaran winked at her. "A commercial myth! Don't disappoint me by buying into it."

Madeline was puzzled and about to ask more questions, but Ciaran raised a finger, gesturing her to hold on. He picked up the handset of the phone at the desk.

"Yes, this is Ciaran. Yes, could you please bring it up here? Also, there should be a fax waiting for me. My assistant Lindsay would have gotten it by now. He's in the Courtyard room. Could you bring me the document as well? Thank you. In the Queen Suite. Yes. Thanks."

Ciaran turned around, smiling at Madeline.

"I didn't know what you like for breakfast, so I ordered the whole lot. The doctor said you can have solid food when you wake. Also . . ."

"Hold on a sec. What's going on here? What happened

last night?" Madeline gestured widely. Everything was confusing to her at the moment.

"I should ask these questions, Madeline. What in God's name were you doing in Fosse Way at that time of night? Your phone sent out a distress signal to me."

"How? It was dead when I was desperate to use it."

"There's a chip in your phone. You're using my company's phone, remember? And don't stress, I wasn't monitoring your whereabouts. It's a standard function in all company phones. Based on changing operating conditions and a lot of other variables, if the phone detects that the user is in possible danger, it will send distress signals to the central operator. I coded your signals to be sent to my phone instead of our operator."

"Got it! And thank you for coming after me."

"You didn't exactly give me any other options," Ciaran murmured. "You know what your logs looked like? Again, it's standard data, I'm not spying on you. You went from London to Mortlake, then straight to the Roman Road during the severe storm warning hours. Then you circled on and off the ancient path, and on and off the road for hours. When I located you, you flew off a wall. Were you practicing for the Grand Prix?"

Ciaran looked at Madeline gently, but there was no amusement in his eyes.

"The Roman soldiers chased me," Madeline explained. She might have hallucinated it, but that was the only piece of information she had and could give at the moment. *I sound like a lunatic*, she thought.

Ciaran gave Madeline a blank stare. He jammed his hands in his pockets and rolled up slightly onto the balls of his feet. Madeline knew that signaled a sarcastic remark was coming. But somehow, he swallowed it before it came out.

Someone knocked on the door. Ciaran opened it to allow the staff to push in a breakfast tray—or a breakfast feast, by Madeline's gauge.

"I'll take this. Thanks." Ciaran took a piece of paper with one hand and grabbed a parcel that looked like clean clothes on coat hangers, wrapped in plastic, with the other. He walked to a wall cabinet to hang up the clothes, as if this was his room.

Madeline stared. Those were her clothes he was handling. She looked down. She was wearing a comfortable white robe. And she was pretty sure by now that underneath the robe was nothing but her skin.

Ciaran glanced quickly at the fax he held in his hand. Looking as if he had seen what he wanted to see, he put the piece of paper on the desk. Then he turned toward Madeline. "The bathroom is there." He pointed to a door in the corner of the room. Then he reached out his hand. "Would you like a hand to get up? Although you had no internal injuries, you had a minor concussion last night. The doctor said you might feel a bit queasy this morning."

Madeline narrowed her eyes, looking down at her robe and then up at Ciaran. "The doctor?"

"Doctor Thomas is our family doctor. He'll follow up this morning to make sure everything is okay."

Madeline looked down again to her robe and back up at Ciaran. She was in a hotel, a private doctor had examined her last night, and in her delirium, she had objected to going to the hospital.

Who exactly had put her in this robe?

Madeline remembered her situation. "I've got to go. I need to be back in London." Zen was coming at any time, and she'd found nothing to show him.

"You're not leaving until you tell me just what happened yesterday. I need answers, Madeline. You can't just brush this off and leave." Ciaran's tone was firm and authoritative.

"I've told you all I know. Look, Ciaran, I appreciate you rescuing me last night, but I really have to go. Right now."

Ciaran stared into her eyes. "You said Roman soldiers chased you. Just so you know, they didn't use guns in that era." His eyes were intense now with a hint of anger.

"Guns? What guns?"

There was a knock on the door.

"That must be Doctor Thomas." Ciaran strode to the door and opened it to let the doctor in.

The man entering the room looked more like a kind grandfather than a doctor. Ciaran fetched a chair and put it next to Madeline's bed so that Doctor Thomas could sit down. Then he went to a corner of the room to answer an incoming call on his cell phone.

"How are you feeling this morning, Madeline?" asked the doctor.

"Just aching a bit. But I feel fine. Thanks for checking on me last night."

"Based on my visual examination, there are no internal injuries. However, I'd like to run a scanner through your body to confirm. Ideally, we should do a head scan as well. But that has to be done at the hospital or at our private lab."

Embarrassment rushed through her. Her entire body had been examined last night, and she didn't even remember it.

"Madeline?"

"Huh?"

"The scan will be quick and gentle. It's better to be safe than sorry." Doctor Thomas looked at her calmly, like a father. Something tugged at her heart. Yes, he was like the father she thought she should have.

"Who was here last night when you examined me?"

Doctor Thomas smiled. "Only Ciaran and myself. There wasn't an army of people in this room if that's what you're worried about." Madeline caught a flash of sorrow in the doctor's eyes.

"I'm feeling fine right now. I'm pretty sure of it." Madeline wiggled her toes underneath the blanket and did a quick mental scan of herself. She did feel fine.

Ciaran finished his phone call and came to the bed.

"No scanning?" Ciaran asked.

"No, she won't agree to it." Doctor Thomas shook his head with fatherly disapproval. Then he turned to Ciaran. "Lindsay was kind enough to deliver my medical bag this morning. So it's time to take your bullet out."

"Bullet? You were shot?" Madeline sat upright in the bed.

CHAPTER 19

"Just a scratch." Ciaran smiled.

"No, it's not. The LeBlanc's painkiller is top of the line, but you can't rely on it any longer. And you can't carry a bullet in your shoulder for more than twelve hours—even one hour is too long for my liking," Doctor Thomas said.

"The Roman soldiers shot at you?" Madeline's voice was shaky.

Ciaran looked at her without a response. Madeline looked at Doctor Thomas, knowing how weird she sounded.

"Don't worry, Madeline. I've worked for the LeBlancs for more than thirty years, and I've heard some very unusual things," Doctor Thomas commented.

"All right," Ciaran compromised, "how long do you need?"

"Three hours."

"I don't have three hours. I have to be in France for an important meeting this afternoon."

"Two hours then."

"Twenty minutes is all I can give you."

"It's surgery, Ciaran. The bullet is in your shoulder, and the wound is deep. Without the scanner, I don't even know exactly where the bullet is. It might not be just a flesh wound, as you seem to think. The strong painkiller would numb your senses."

"Half an hour. You're a good doctor. I trust you can do it." Ciaran grabbed his jacket that was resting on the reading chair. "Let's go."

"Go where?" Madeline asked.

"My room, of course!" Ciaran answered, cocking an eyebrow.

"No, no, oh no! Do it right here!"

Ciaran looked at the doctor, puzzled, then looked at Madeline. "I beg your pardon?"

"We can talk after Doctor Thomas has scooped the bullet out of you. It'll save time, you'll see. It's just minor surgery. I'll explain to you all about last night. You should be fine talking while he's working." Madeline raised an eyebrow in challenge.

You got to see me naked, and you got the doctor to work on me? Well, it's time for payback. Madeline knew it was mean of her, but she couldn't help it.

"When you're finished with your surgery, I'll be gone. I have to be back in London. Right now," Madeline added.

"If you need things done within half an hour, I could use some help," Doctor Thomas said in support of Madeline's suggestion.

Ciaran was reluctant for a second, then nodded. "All right, no anesthesia, Doctor Thomas. Just numb it."

Madeline got up from the bed quickly, prepared for her role as nurse. Ciaran took his shirt off. In front of her was an exquisite, well-toned, and sculptured set of muscles on a slender body that God must have created when he was in a very, very good mood. Madeline pretended to cinch her robe.

Drooling in front of a guy is not attractive, Madeline. Preserve some of your dignity, she told herself.

Doctor Thomas removed the bandage from Ciaran's wound. Madeline gasped when she saw it. A slash of guilt cut into her. That could have been *her* bullet.

"Lie down in the bed for me, will you, Ciaran?"

Ciaran kicked his shoes off and obeyed Doctor Thomas without hesitation, showing that he just wanted to get his procedure over with as soon as possible. Madeline had expected that the humiliation of being handled in front of her would be so enormous that Ciaran would forget to ask her any questions. But apparently, he didn't miss a trick.

He lay on his side, his back facing outward so that Doctor Thomas could work on him. Ciaran looked at Madeline, who was standing on the opposite side of the bed, her hands in the pockets of her hotel robe.

"There were no Roman soldiers, Madeline. But you were running from *someone.* When I found you and managed to land the rescue helicopter, you were running away from me. You wouldn't stop. Then after I'd gotten to you, bullets rained down on us. I couldn't see anyone, but I'm sure it was more than one person. When my rescue team approached us, they found no one, but they did discover several bullet casings by the ditch."

Ciaran winced as he felt a prick from the needle.

"I can see the bullet," Doctor Thomas informed him. "I'm numbing you now."

Ciaran nodded slightly in acknowledgement.

Madeline cleared her throat. "I was looking for John Dee's tomb, but I'm not after gold if that's what you're thinking . . ."

"I'm not drawing any conclusions yet."

"An old woman at Mortlake . . ."

"Mrs. Hanson?"

"Yes, you know her?"

"Yes, but we no longer have any association. I sought her consultation on natural medicine. I was told that people were looking for John Dee's grave, and Mrs. Hanson claimed she knew where it is. But people came to ask for her advice, and they were never seen again."

"Well, obviously she sent the Roman soldiers after them!" Madeline exclaimed.

"If you're not after the gold like the others, why do you need to find John Dee's grave? Does it have anything to do with your friend's computer game?"

"Look Ciaran, it could have been worse than a bullet in your shoulder. I . . ."

"This bullet is nothing. I need the truth, Madeline."

"Stay still, Ciaran," Doctor Thomas warned.

"Sorry," Ciaran muttered, his eyes flashing with anger but calming quickly.

First, Stephen took a bullet. Now Ciaran. Who will be next? Madeline bit her lips, unsure what to say.

"Madeline, I need answers."

She nodded, those deep gray eyes telling her he was not going to let this slide. "Yes, this has to do with the computer game my friend, Jo, developed. She was kidnapped. If I can't find out who is playing as an avatar in her game, they're going to kill Jo." A tear ran down Madeline's face.

Ciaran shook his head, trying to stay alert. "Who are *they*?"

"Jo's boss. The guy owns a game development company. I don't know why he wanted me to find John Dee's grave."

"What's the avatar?" Madeline flickered in front of Ciaran, starting to fade. Her voice seemed to echo in his head. "Damn it. God damn it, Doctor Thomas." Ciaran sat up, but then flopped face down back on to the bed.

Doctor Thomas looked at Madeline and shrugged. "I'm going to need more than half an hour. Please help me straighten him up."

Madeline climbed onto the bed and turned Ciaran so he lay on his side. His face had gone lax, and his skin burned. "He has a fever," she said.

Doctor Thomas nodded. "Yes, without the painkiller, he'd be in very poor shape. You may want to call his assistant, Lindsay, and tell him that Ciaran won't make it to the meeting this afternoon."

Madeline followed his instructions. She skimmed through Ciaran's address book and called.

"This is Madeline. Doctor Thomas asked me to let you know that Ciaran won't make it to the meeting this afternoon . . . Inform his family? . . ." Madeline saw Doctor Thomas shook his head. "No, no need to . . . He'd need . . . ah . . ." Madeline saw Doctor Thomas mime the time He'd need until tomorrow. So no more work today. Okay?"

Madeline hung up the phone. "Lindsay said to tell you he'd take care of Robert's family."

Doctor Thomas nodded. Noticing the flash of pain that came across Doctor Thomas's face, Madeline caught him giving her another unusual glance. She pressed, "Who's Robert, Doctor Thomas?"

Doctor Thomas was reluctant, but not for long. "Ciaran's head of security. He wasn't as lucky last night. He was shot in the head and died instantly. No pain. But he just had a daughter born last month. There will be a lot of pain for the living."

Madeline felt a heavy weight on her chest. It was hard to breathe. It was exactly the same heavy weight she felt when Mrs. Hanson mentioned her grief. How could she have been grieving *before* this happened? If that was her psychic ability, it certainly wasn't an ability she wanted to have.

She opened the window for some air, but when the cold wind rushed into the room, she closed it quickly. Someone died in an attempt to rescue her last night. What if the bullet hadn't just been in Ciaran's shoulder but somewhere fatal? Would there be more killing when Zen figured out she had lied to him?

Doctor Thomas looked at Ciaran, who was sleeping like a baby. "Robert and Ciaran were like brothers. Ciaran was really angry at himself last night . . ."

"At himself? Why not at me? Wasn't it my fault?"

Doctor Thomas stared at Madeline. "Your fault? No! Ciaran was angry at the cowardice, at the actions of those who shot at you from the dark. Robert was his people, his family. I know Ciaran. He'll never let this go. But before he does something about it, he'll need proper rest."

Doctor Thomas packed up his medical bag and shook his head. "I have a feeling that this one is going to be a long haul."

"I was blackmailed for information. They shot at my friend in New York. Now, they're shooting at me, and they ended up killing an innocent man, and almost killed Ciaran. Now I don't have what they want. They might kill my friend tomorrow. It's all my fault," Madeline cried. "It's what I did. It's my bad karma." Her suppressed emotions came out in a storm of tears.

Doctor Thomas held her and stroked her back like a father until the weeping subsided. "I don't know you, Madeline," he said. "But I have a feeling that you're much like Ciaran. So I'll say to you what I've always said to him. You can't take responsibility for other people's actions. You might have done something in the past that you're not proud of. But that does not translate into what happens to others. Robert's death cannot be because of Ciaran's bad karma. Your friend's fate cannot be your fault. Ciaran never listens to me. He's been stubborn since he was a kid. But I hope you'll give my advice some consideration."

Doctor Thomas headed toward the door while Madeline wiped the tears from her face.

"Robert's death came down really hard on Ciaran last night. I didn't need three hours to operate. I just wanted him to rest. I put him on some sleep-inducing drugs. In his normal condition, it would only give him a couple of hours sleep. But given what happened last night, I don't know how long the drug will knock him out. When he comes to, he would have any negative reactions to the anaesthetic. He's allergic to some of the ingredients in the sedative. Because of that, he might throw a tantrum. I'll leave that for you to handle."

"What? Me? No—"

"Yes, you can. No one has ever made him do what he didn't want to do. But you did it today. I am sure one of his little tantrums will be no big deal to you." The doctor smiled and left the room.

CHAPTER 20

*M*adeline used Ciaran's phone to ask Lindsay to arrange a new cell phone for her. Within fifteen minutes, the phone was delivered to her door.

She used the new phone to access her email. As predicted, there was a message from Zen. The message read, "We had a date and you stood me up. I'm with Jo now in London. Looking forward to seeing you again. Jo says hi, by the way. She misses you. Also, thanks for sending your friend to pay me a visit. Please send him my regards. Hope to catch up soon. Love from Zen."

He didn't know what she was up to. As long as she didn't talk to him, he wouldn't do anything drastic and wouldn't hurt Jo. She was his only bargaining power.

Madeline sent Stephen an email asking his whereabouts and got an instant message back from his email saying he was still in transit.

She made herself a cup of coffee. The caffeine jolted her system and made her feel a lot better.

The longer she could keep Zen in the dark, the better it would be.

The current issue for her right now was the man lying on her bed. He had taken a bullet for her and had lost a friend for her. Yet they were total strangers.

Madeline went over to the bed, laying her hand on Ciaran's forehead to check his temperature. She was pleased to find that it had gone down. She tucked away a strand of stray hair on his forehead.

She couldn't help it but trace her finger over his lips. He looked so peaceful when he slept. *How many women have kissed those lips?* she wondered and shook her head. *Mental slap.*

She glanced at the clock. It had been four hours since he had fallen asleep—double the amount the doctor expected. "You're not invincible, after all," she said quietly and went back to the desk, using the internet from the phone to do more work.

When she next looked up, it had become dark, and she was famished.

On the bed, Ciaran stirred.

Madeline picked up the hotel phone and ordered dinner. Shortly afterward, Ciaran opened his eyes. She sat at his bedside and smiled. He didn't smile back.

He tried to sit up and was successful on his second attempt.

Ciaran stood from the bed. He swayed with dizziness and leaned against the wall to get his balance. Madeline watched and said nothing. Ciaran grabbed his shirt and walked toward the door.

She stopped him on his way and handed him a couple of pills and a glass of water. "Painkillers. You'll need them."

Ciaran grunted out a thank you and downed the pills. As soon as the water hit his throat, he had only enough time to put down the glass of water before he ran to the bathroom to vomit. When he emerged, he looked pale as a ghost. Doctor Thomas was right, Ciaran hadn't handled the anesthesia well. He put on his shirt and walked toward the door of the room. Remembering his shoes, he walked toward the bed where he had kicked them off earlier.

Dinner arrived just in time to break the awkward silence.

Damn it, she thought. She was usually a lot better at handling situations like this.

"Hungry?" she asked with a smile.

Ciaran shook his head. "I should go back to my room."

"Why don't you have something to eat? Doctor Thomas warned me the anesthesia wouldn't agree with you, but you needed it. He needed to do a proper surgery, and you needed to rest."

Ciaran gave Madeline a blank stare then smiled. "You think I'm grumpy because of that? What else did Doctor Thomas tell you?"

"I'm sorry." She couldn't find more words so she settled with those. "I'm sorry about Robert. I'm very sorry you've lost your friend because of me, Ciaran."

His eyes darkened. "It's not your fault." His voice was so low it was almost a growl. He backed out, nodded a goodbye to Madeline, and strode toward the door.

She grabbed him from behind and held him.

Ciaran paused.

She kissed his shoulder. Jo always said Madeline's sultry voice was her best asset. She might as well utilize it now. She murmured, "I'm so sorry, Ciaran, I truly am."

She felt his body tense up and turned him around. She wasn't sure whether it was what she said or her voice that captured him. She swiped a strand of hair out of his face. Black hair framing the face of a dark angel that was looking down at her. "I think it was my fault," she said.

He reacted, but before he could say anything, her mouth was on his.

Her kiss was persuasive. She could feel his muscles relax a bit. Madeline stopped the kiss. "Somehow you think you're responsible for what happened. You could have ignored the distress signal from my phone. But you didn't. And your friend died because of that."

Ciaran said nothing.

She kissed him again. This time, the kiss was deeper.

"If you don't accept that it was my fault, then you can't say it's your fault either." She looked into his intense gray eyes which were full of inexplicable emotions.

Ciaran slid one hand around her neck and the other at her lower back, almost lifting her off the ground, and kissed her. Strong and hard. Every muscle in her body quivered. Then he released her. "It wasn't your fault. And thank you for the sympathy kiss. I appreciate it." He nodded a goodbye and walked straight out the door.

She paused and stared at the wall.

"What did he just say?" she thought and cursed once she'd realized he had left the room. She stormed out after him. She had to let him know that she would follow him all the way to hell and back. It was her genuine intention, she was . . .

Madeline looked around the long, dark corridor of the fifteenth century castle. She had no idea where Ciaran's room was.

She heard a thud and realized that the door of her room had slammed behind her. Here she was, standing in a castle, wearing a hotel robe and nothing else—and without a key to get back into the room.

CHAPTER 21

She tiptoed across the cold tiled floor of the foyer, through a dark, cobblestoned courtyard to the reception desk and asked for a key to get back into her room.

"I'll be fine getting back by myself. Thank you," she said to the concierge who offered to escort her back to her room.

"Very well ma'am. And the King's suite is on the top floor, at the end of the East Wing."

"I'm in the Queen's suite."

"I know, ma'am. But I thought you . . . Oh, I beg your pardon . . ." The concierge nodded a goodbye and scurried out of the reception room as fast as he could while Madeline glared at him.

IN HIS ROOM, Ciaran yanked off his shirt and tossed it onto the bed. He went into the bathroom to try to get a look at his back in the mirror. He peeled the bandage off so hard that the new wound started to bleed again.

He could feel the warm blood trickling down his back. He braced his hands on the basin and closed his eyes to absorb the sensation of it.

Blood had been spilled, and he had to remember that. He'd never forgive those who harmed the people he loved and protected.

He turned on the tap to let the cold water run and then dipped his head in the running water. It didn't stop his blood from boiling with fury. Rage.

There were two people in his life who had seen and condemned his demon. One was his father, and the other one was, ironically, Robert.

He looked at himself in the mirror and could see the fury burning in his eyes, in his soul.

He made medicine, and he was one of the best. Yet his father died with illness before he could say a parting word to him. And Robert? What could he have done to save him from a bullet in the head?

Through his haze of anger, Ciaran heard a knock on the door. He ignored it.

Then came a bang.

He brushed his hair back with his fingers, mumbled some profanity, and, leaving the water and blood to drip down his body, yanked open the door.

In front of him was Madeline in her hotel robe and bare feet—and if he was not mistaken, she was angry. Ciaran braced his arm on the door frame, more to maintain his balance than to appear intimidating.

Madeline had her hands on her hips, and he knew from the set of that beautiful mouth that venom was coming his way.

She looked him up and down, and then her arms

flopped down to her sides, and her big brown eyes watered.

Ciaran cursed on the inside. "You're here to give me another round of sympathy kisses? Or did you want to upgrade it to charity sex?" he asked.

Madeline snarled and flew at him. He caught her hand in the air before it hit his face. He could have let it slip and taken the slap. He certainly needed it.

"Leave me alone, Madeline," Ciaran said and retreated inside.

"Oh for pity's sake . . ." Madeline said and shoved him from behind so hard that he almost fell on his face. "You want to bleed to death, go ahead. I'll stand here and watch. But I'm going nowhere." She kicked the door closed.

That was it. His rage was coming on full-force. Ciaran stood up. "Get away from me. I don't want to hurt you."

Madeline kept her stance, blocking the door. Ciaran tried to yank it open to shove her out, but she was a lot stronger than he thought. Or maybe he was a lot weaker. He snarled and walked back into the room. The next thing he knew, a tray of crystal and a decanter flew across the room.

"Keep your distance from Madeline, or you'll hurt her" was the only thought in his mind at the moment. His father had been the only person who could help him control his rage. But his father wasn't here.

Now, he had to destroy.

Had to burn.

Had to ruin.

The fury clawed at him. It was a battle between Ciaran and the inanimate objects in the room, with the objects at a distinct disadvantage in the fight. He flew at a cabinet. The cabinet doors cracked and crumbled, one after the other. He crushed the bedside table. He destroyed everything and anything within those four walls. Then he stared at the mirror in the bathroom.

He felt her hands pulling him back from behind. He heard her beg, "Please stop, Ciaran. That's enough."

He fell to the floor, exhausted, and Madeline grabbed a towel to stanch the bleeding from his wound. He got up, staggered to the bed, and dropped face down onto a pillow, letting the fury wash over him.

It was strong and irresistible, and there was nothing he could do about it. Then he felt the warmth of her hands, wiping the blood from his back.

In his near delirium, he reached out and grabbed her hand. "Please stay."

CHAPTER 22

A few hours passed. Madeline still stared at the broken cabinet doors. Lying in the bed in Ciaran's arms, she felt every movement of his body, his energy. Their bodies fit like two pieces of a jigsaw puzzle that were meant to be next to each other.

What would the big picture be like? Her life? His life? And everyone else around them? Would they make a complete picture? Would the other pieces fit to one another?

His heart rate had slowed, the pain that was seeping out of his pores had subdued, and he was once again peacefully asleep. Then he stirred. Madeline propped up on her elbow and rolled away from Ciaran. He opened his eyes, then sprung to his feet.

He looked her up and down. "Madeline, did I …"

"No. I didn't offer anything, and you didn't take anything."

He let out a sign of relief, and looked around the room, or what was left of it. "Did I hurt you?"

"No. But the furniture wouldn't say the same."

"I asked you to leave. Why didn't you?"

"I thought you were going to turn into a werewolf, so I was curious," she joked. "But I didn't see any paws or fur. Plus, you needed a hugging pillow." She shrugged.

Ciaran stared at her. He shook his head and smiled, but his eyes suggested a laugh on the inside. He tilted her chin up and gazed into her big brown eyes. He rubbed the dimple on her left cheek with his thumb. "I'm sorry for what I said before."

"What did you say? I can't remember."

"I have issues with my anger, Madeline. When the rage comes, I know I'll say and do things I'll regret. It rarely comes but when it does, I don't have any control over it."

"What about an anger management program?"

Ciaran laughed and shook his head. Once the laughter had died, his eyes were once again intense. "The problem isn't psychological."

She should have known. The energy of his fury was strong and primal. It came in waves, and it was so catastrophic that she saw it in her psychic mind. The weight of his grief blasted at her like an explosion. This was what Mrs. Hanson had talked about. It wasn't Robert's death but what came afterward. It wasn't what the death had taken away but what the living carried with them. His grief was contagious, and now she was carrying the same baggage because of her psychic ability.

"Are you hungry?" she asked.

"Starving."

"Well, there's an absolute feast in my room that used to be dinner. But given that it's now three in the morning, I'd call it breakfast. Interested?"

Ciaran tucked a strand of hair behind her ear and kissed her forehead. "I'd love to."

$\sim$

LATER ON, after Madeline told Ciaran everything, he looked at her over the rim of the glass of red wine, contemplating, and smiled to himself.

"What?" Madeline asked.

"Regarding this Stephen character, have you ever considered giving him a chance?"

"To what?"

Ciaran chuckled. "He likes you."

Madeline laughed. "Stephen is harmless!"

"Uhmm!" Ciaran smiled and said nothing, but made some kind of sound that Madeline was pretty sure meant he didn't believe her.

"Don't call Stephen a character—he's a real cop!"

"I see! On that note, would you bring him into this later on?"

"Not if I could help it."

"You meant if 'I' could help?"

Right. Madeline rolled her eyes. *Egotistical clash of the male species.* She said nothing, just smiled. She thought that would be best.

"Why don't you tell Zen that I'm the White Knight? I can talk to him and make him believe me. Then we can arrange a fake John Dee's tomb for him to dig up. When we've got him snug in our trap, we can politely hand him over to Stephen-the-cop and get Jo out of trouble."

Ciaran plainly played out the strategy out loud while leaning back in his chair, swirling the wine in his glass, and looking as if he was playing a harmless game of Monopoly.

Madeline said nothing. He made it sound so easy. *Jo wasn't the only one good at games*, Madeline thought.

"Don't like the plan?"

"Oh, yes, of course. It's perfect . . . So you don't think there's a real John Dee's tomb?"

"There must be one somewhere, but I'm not interested in his gold, nor do I have any desire to dig up a grave."

"Zen is a computer game fanatic. You think you can make him believe you?"

Ciaran smiled. "I'm an excellent player."

"Have you ever gotten into trouble with the police?"

Ciaran kept sipping this wine.

"Just a rhetorical question," Madeline muttered and smiled, looking at Ciaran. Her prince had returned to his full, magnificent form, post-surgery. "What . . . what are you going to do about Robert?"

His face was unfathomable. "We'll pay his family a visit." He stood up to leave the room.

"I don't think your room is inhabitable at the moment."

"You slept on my bed before!"

"I didn't. But you did."

He nodded. "I'll arrange another room."

She arched an eyebrow. "Another hotel room?"

"We can come back to One Hyde Park. I've got it reserved for a couple of days."

"A couple of days! Don't you have a home? A permanent address?"

He gazed into her eyes. She couldn't read his emotion. Whatever skills she'd obtained in her day job didn't work on him. Her psychic ability gave her nothing but his contagious grief.

"I have a number of addresses. They're permanent because they are mine. But none of them truly qualifies as a home. The apartment at One Hyde Park will do for a week,"

"Then what?"

He shoved his hands into his pockets. "Then we'll see." Then he turned around and walked back to the mess he called his room.

CHAPTER 23

*T*he lush carpeted corridor of LeBlanc Pharmaceuticals unfolded before Madeline as she walked alongside Ciaran to his corporate wing. People greeted him, some with a smile, some with words, and some with a courteous nod. But they all had one thing in common—respect. But it wasn't respect based on the power and intimidation that money could buy. Madeline didn't need her psychic ability to be aware of the aura around Ciaran. Something about him was insanely humane but yet distant and powerful at the same time.

She would be scared if she got on his bad side. None of the people here had seen his rage—she was sure of it.

The corridor opened to a reception area at the entrance where a large secretary's desk was located. The secretary was busy on the phone when Ciaran and Madeline entered. At the corner of the room, Madeline saw the most gorgeous dog ever, fast asleep on the carpet on his back with four legs in the air. A bowl of dog food was tucked in the corner, and the most of the food had been spilled all over the carpet. Bags of extra food and toys were scattered all over the floor of the 'dog quarters'.

"What we have here?" Madeline asked.

The puppy woke instantly as Ciaran approached. "He jumped into my car when I was stuck in a traffic jam," Ciaran said as he crouched and reached his hand out to the dog. The puppy dove into Ciaran, wagging his tail in excitement and licking Ciaran's hand. Ciaran frowned at the sign the puppy wore around his neck, which stated: "I am Ciaran's dog. Please treat me nicely."

That would explain all the food and toys the dog had. The smile faded from Ciaran's face. He put the dog down and approached the secretary, who had finished on the phone.

"Ciaran," she greeted.

Ciaran smiled. "Good morning, Lily. This is my friend, Madeline. I have some changes in my schedule. Could you cancel my meetings in France for the next couple of days? Ask Lindsay to address all questions."

"Yes, Ciaran." Lily typed quickly on the computer.

"And take the dog to the pound," Ciaran said, wrapping his arm around Madeline's waist to lead her to his office.

"Excuse me? Ciaran!" Lily asked.

Ciaran stopped on the way and turned around, "I said, take the dog to the pound. I don't want to see it anymore."

Lily's eyes teared up. "Yes, Ciaran."

When the office door had closed behind him, Ciaran went to the desk and made a call. Madeline sat down in a chair and waited. Ciaran finished the call.

"Would you like something to drink? I've arranged a car. We can go to Robert's and then drop by Mortlake to visit Mrs. Hanson."

Then he saw the look on Madeline's face. "What, Madeline?"

"If you want Lily to adopt the dog, you should just ask her. I'm sure she will."

Ciaran sat down at this desk. He didn't smile, but his eyes twinkled.

He's intrigued. Madeline smiled and patted herself on the back.

"I prefer flexibility." He smiled now and stood up from his chair to move around to the other side of his desk. Her stomach quivered and spasmed at an alarming level. Then he stopped on his way.

The computer screen on his desk flashed and turned itself on. He frowned. Madeline stood up, came around to where he was, and looked at the monitor. The screen was filled with static symbols. It flashed once, twice, and then some text appeared. *"It's time, Ciaran. The enemies are nearby."* Then the screen flashed again and turned itself off.

Ciaran dove at the keyboard and typed frantically. For a while, he sank into his work and didn't look up once. Madeline sat in the chair, waiting. Then he stopped, turned it off, and stared at the blank screen.

"Hacker?" Madeline asked.

He shook his head.

"So it's internal then?"

He swivelled his chair around, looking at her. His intense gray eyes were darkened, but he said nothing.

"Police?" Madeline guessed. "Spy? Cyber terrorist? Fanatic? Serial killer?" Madeline had her hands on her hips. "Vampire? Witch? Werewolf? Angel? Or demon? Come on, Ciaran!"

Ciaran gazed at the computer screen. "Extraterrestrial," he said.

"It's . . . it's from aliens?"

Ciaran approached the cabinet at corner of the room and opened it. He drew out a decanter of scotch, and poured it into a crystal glass. He gestured to ask if Madeline wanted some. She shook her head.

"You knew this? You weren't surprised?" she asked.

Ciaran sipped the spirits and stared out the window.

"You said your rage wasn't psychological. Are you—?"

"No, I'm human, if that's what you're asking."

Madeline nodded. "Why did the aliens say I'm your enemy?" She raised her voice.

"What? No. They weren't referring to you." Ciaran put the glass down and walked around the desk to approach Madeline.

"It has to be me. Someone gave me a mysterious note. Then I ran into you. Then you got shot, and Robert got killed. Disaster. I can only bring you disaster." A tear rolled down her face. "I have to leave."

Ciaran blocked her at the door. He grabbed her shoulders and directed her back inside. He lifted her and sat her on his desk. Then he embraced her, hard. His arms were like a vice—there was no way she could wriggle her way out of his grasp. For a while, she could feel his muscles vibrating along with her emotions.

Then he released her. He kissed her forehead, lifted her chin up, and looked into her eyes. "You're not my enemy, Madeline. I have many of them, and you're not on the list."

"I lied to you about the game hacking."

He snorted. "You're an amateur when it comes to lying, Madeline. I trust you, and I don't trust people easily."

"Why?"

"Because no one that I've taken to One Hyde Park before has ever noticed I don't have a TV, and that the apartment wasn't my home."

She smiled.

"Not a single woman before you has ever noticed that the meals I served them were takeout. All they saw in that apartment was the shine and the attraction of money and power."

She laughed. "Exactly how many girls have you taken there?"

He smiled. "And none of them have ever cared how many others I've taken there." He kissed her lips lightly. "You know very well I could have forced myself on you last night. You know I could have done the unthinkable. Yet you stayed with me."

He deepened their kiss, and her head started to spin. She spoke, her breath quickening. "Because you asked me . . ."

He roamed his hands up and down her arms. "What else?"

"You needed a hugging pillow . . ."

His hands were under her blouse. She pulled at his shirt, untucking it from his waist. "What else?" he asked.

"Because . . . you let a puppy into your car!"

He stopped kissing her and started laughing. When his laughter finally subsided to chuckles, he said, "I have many secrets, Madeline. A lot of them you're better off not knowing. But if any of my secrets got you tangled up in my mess, I won't let anything happen to you." He tucked a stray hair behind her ear and rubbed his thumb on her dimple.

"So if all this wasn't because of your secrets, I'll be just another girl you took into your luxurious apartment?" She hopped down to the floor.

He grabbed her and put her back up on the desk.

"Without my mess, I'm sure I don't have anything to hold you, Madeline."

She frowned.

"You're a very complicated woman."

"It comes with the job." She saw his eyes twinkle again.

"I won't let anything happen to you," he repeated.

"Same goes for me." She hopped off his desk once again and strode toward the door. She didn't look back, but she knew she had made his eyes twinkle again. She hadn't intended to do that to impress him. But somehow, there was a rhythm in this thought and his emotion that she could tap into.

She felt him. And somehow, she knew he felt her, too.

CHAPTER 24

*T*he town was charming, but she just felt something wrong was about to crash down on Ciaran and her. Ciaran parked his car in the yard of a cottage in Stow-on-the-Wold. The house was as cozy and charming as the ancient town in which it was located. Ciaran pushed the door open and walked straight into the house.

This used to be his home! Madeline thought.

A woman stormed out from the side room. She clung to Ciaran and sobbed. Ciaran embraced her and murmured something that Madeline knew was more than typical condolences. There was no formality between them. He held the woman tightly and said nothing until her weeping abated.

"This is my friend, Madeline Roux. Laurent Chandler, Robert's wife." Laurent Chandler was in her late thirties and quietly attractive.

"I'm very sorry for your loss, Mrs. Chandler."

Laurent smiled. "Laurent, it is! Would you like a cup of tea?"

Laurent led them to the room at the back of the house. The room was warm with candlelight. The winter sun didn't shed much light into the room, particularly on a grim day like this. Robert's coffin lay in the middle, and his picture stood quietly on a stand next to it. Robert Chandler was a sturdy looking man in his early forties. He looked formidable with a strong face, brown hair, and honest eyes. Ciaran stood still, looking at the picture. Beneath his calm expression was the unspeakable pain that Madeline understood.

Laurent came into the room with the baby in her arms. She gave her to Ciaran. He held the baby gently, kissing her forehead as if she would break like crystal. Then he gave the baby back to Laurent.

"Were you comfortable with Lindsay's arrangements?" Ciaran asked.

Laurent looked at Ciaran. Her eyes were dry now and filled with the affection of a sister. "That was all Robert would have wished for. He'd be pleased. Doctor Thomas put through an official record of accidental death. Everything was handled smoothly. Thank you."

"You thank me for this?"

"Yes. And Robert would thank you for what you've done for us."

"I'll find the answer, Laurent. I will find the answer for all of this."

"Please don't mix it with vengeance, Ciaran. Robert's death was part of the job he took on with you."

"He had no such duty, Laurent. There is no money in the world that could give his girl back her father, give you back your husband . . . and me . . . back my friend. Had I known . . ."

"You didn't know, Ciaran. You didn't know, and let's keep it at that."

Laurent looked at Madeline. Madeline couldn't understand how a newly grieving widow could have had such warmth in her eyes. *If she knew it was me who had caused Ciaran to go to Fosse Way—and hence the death of her husband—would she still have that warmth in her eyes right now?*

"Ciaran," Laurent continued, "Robert would have been happy to see you open up for a new life. Ten years is enough to forgive."

"But not enough to forget, Laurent. Never enough," Ciaran growled and sounded as if he didn't care the conversation to go further in that direction.

Just before Ciaran and Madeline left, she saw the blue dots hovering in the air. She wasn't sure whether they hovered around her, Ciaran, Laurent, or the coffin.

She hadn't told Ciaran about her psychic ability. *Why were the blue dots hovering here?* Madeline shook her head, trying to will the thought out of her head.

"What's the matter, Madeline?"

"Huh?" she asked and realized they had left the house and now were standing in front of Ciaran's car. She didn't know where to begin to tell Ciaran about the blue dots.

Whenever she saw the blue dots, something unfortunate would happen.

Just let it slide for now, she thought, shook her head, and got into the car.

CHAPTER 25

The street was just the same as it was when Madeline had last seen it. Ciaran parked a block away from Mrs. Hanson's cottage. Madeline knew he could park right at the front, but she had trained herself not to ask questions.

As soon as they entered the front yard of the cottage, Mrs. Hanson appeared mysteriously on the doorstep. Had she known they were coming?

"It's good to see you again, Ciaran. What did this old woman do to deserve a visit?"

She stepped down from the steps to the lawn. Her weird earrings jingled, making an unpleasant sound with her every step. Madeline wished it would stop as it made her head ring.

The woman looked at Madeline. "I'm glad to see you again, too!"

"You know why we're here, Mrs. Hanson. I know you're disappointed to see her alive."

"I don't know what you're talking about, Ciaran. This

young lady was just here asking for directions a couple of days ago. She must have found what she wanted, given my instructions. Aren't you grateful for my help, Madeline?"

"How do you know my name? I didn't introduce myself."

Madeline remembered the jingle of Mrs. Hanson's earrings now. She had heard that sound when she'd hallucinated about the Roman soldiers. They were the sounds that made her head ring, her eyes droop, and ended up with her driving into the walls.

Madeline grabbed Ciaran's arm, pulling him backward. "Her earrings, the sound of her earrings is what caused my hallucination at the walls. Don't listen to it."

Mrs. Hanson grinned widely, showing her black and rotting teeth.

"They contacted you, didn't they Mrs. Hanson? They've made an appearance." Ciaran advanced on the woman.

Mrs. Hanson grunted out her words. "Greedy people are supposed to die!"

"You don't care about those greedy people. I know what you want. You're as greedy as they are. They killed my friend. Tell me where they are."

The woman laughed. "If I don't tell you, what will you do? Kill this old woman? So much for the gentlemen I used to know? And all that because of this *bitch*?"

"Don't call her names!" Ciaran growled. "Tell me where they are, and I'll leave you in peace."

Mrs. Hanson laughed—a crooked laugh that pulled at the muscles on her face and made it look as if she was in pain. "You think you can blackmail me?"

"I don't think it. I do it. I know where you get the supplies to make your evil drugs. I can stop it right now. With one phone call."

"Don't you dare!" The woman flew at Ciaran and shoved him backward. Madeline darted in front of him and shoved the woman away.

She gave the old woman a stern stare. "He wouldn't hit a woman, but I wouldn't mind a cat fight."

"Try me!" she screamed, but the scream came out more like a croak. She swung her head so that her earrings jingled loudly. Madeline grabbed her ears and stepped back.

Mrs. Hanson shook her arms so that the bells dangling on her beaded wristbands sang as well. The sound from the earrings was the worst, though. Mrs. Hanson looked as if she was dancing.

Ciaran stepped in front of Madeline. "Go to the car and wait for me there," he directed.

"No."

"Go, Madeline!"

Mrs. Hanson swung her earrings more violently. Madeline thought her nose and ears would bleed. She heard Mrs. Hanson laughing. Her laugh was loud now, and the ringing noise pierced her brain like a well-sharpened knife. Thousands of knives. Madeline heard Ciaran calling to her, asking her to leave. She could feel him grabbing her, pulling her away.

The noise was pounding in her head.

No, she wouldn't run. Not from an old woman with weird earrings. The old woman had killed Robert. His blood was on her hands, as well as on Madeline's. In her mind, Madeline saw Robert's widow and his orphan. She remembered now what happened at Fosse Way. What she had seen were not Roman soldiers. They were men with rifles wearing masks. They had bells on their rifles, and clothes that made the same sound.

Madeline shrugged off Ciaran's grip and rushed toward the old woman. She grabbed her dangling earrings and pulled hard. The sound stopped. The woman screamed in pain as blood poured out of her torn ear lobes. Then the old woman grunted, and the sound coming out of her mouth was deep and demonic.

She pulled a knife from beneath her clothing and ran back toward Madeline.

Seeing the flash of the knife, Madeline stepped back, and Ciaran darted toward her from behind. Madeline tripped on a small stone, tumbled, and fell on her back. The old woman growled and jumped on top of Madeline, arcing the knife up in the air and preparing to stab downward.

Ciaran grabbed the old woman's hand. The old woman looked at him as if she had been waiting for just that moment. She didn't jerk her hand out of Ciaran's. It happened in front of Madeline's eyes as if it were a slow-motion movie. The old woman turned the knife and pulled it toward herself, along with Ciaran's hand.

She stabbed the knife deep into her chest.

From the back, Shaun, the gardener, walked out and saw Ciaran's hand still on the hilt of the knife which had been plunged into Mrs. Hanson's body.

"Oh, God! Oh, my God! Mrs. Hanson!" He stumbled backward, fell, and then stood up and ran.

Madeline rolled away. Mrs. Hanson lay on the ground, grinning ghoulishly back at Madeline and Ciaran. She reached her hand up, grabbed Ciaran's shirt, and pulled him down.

"Blood on your hands. Blood in your soul. I curse you, Ciaran . . . for the young soul that died for you . . . It's time. The enemies are coming . . ."

The old woman stared into nothing. Dead eyes.

Ciaran yanked himself free of the woman's grip. Then he just stood there, looking incredulously at the blood on his hands.

CHAPTER 26

"*A*re you okay?" Ciaran held Madeline's shoulders and looked into her eyes while they waited for the elevator in the foyer of One Hyde Park. "You were very quiet on the way back."

She could give him a white lie to get this over and done with, but he had figured out she was lousy in that regard. And those intense gray eyes were so filled with genuine concern and emotion that she would feel like a bitch lying to him.

"Well, it's not every day that I see someone die in front of me. You were shakier than me, though. I pulled *you* from the scene, remember?" She sighed. *I lied to him anyway*, she thought.

He lifted her chin. "On the contrary, you were *too* steady for the situation. And that's what I'm concerned about."

"Hey!" She pushed his hand away. "You think I eat people for breakfast?" She put her hands defensively on her hips. *Damn, should have known he would see that.*

"One day, you'll have to tell me about what happened to you, Madeline."

"Who the hell do you think you are?"

He shrugged.

"My personal life is none of your business." She jabbed a finger at his shoulder.

Ciaran nodded. "Someone is using you to get to me. That's my business, and I'm entitled to know what's relevant. If you don't want me to know about your past, I won't ask again."

She nodded and looked away.

"Lindsay will have a car picking us up in ten minutes. We're going to the police station to give information as witnesses."

"These police, are they yours?"

Ciaran chuckled. "If you mean do they live in our pocket, no. Detective Adamson is a good friend of Lindsay's. We don't bribe, Madeline."

"Why did Mrs. Hanson kill herself? Just for a chance to frame us?"

"It's not her we talked to. Remember how I threatened to cut her supplies with a phone call?"

Madeline nodded.

"I did that to her ten years ago. She no longer makes medicines that require those supplies. So what's running in her head now is like an old tape recorder of behaviour and thought patterns."

Madeline's eyes widened. "You knew it back there? You were testing her?"

"That used to be a woman. But it's not anymore, I'm afraid."

"What? She was abducted by aliens, and they replaced her human brain with a robotic one?"

Ciaran chuckled and shook his head.

"She was possessed by a demon of her past?"

Ciaran grinned. "You have a very unusual thought process, Madeline."

"So tell me!"

"You don't want me to know your stories, so you don't get to know mine."

Damn, Madeline cursed silently.

The elevator opened. At the same time, Madeline's phone buzzed. She glanced at the screen. Unknown ID.

Ciaran nodded. She picked up, and Zen's voice oozed out from the other end of the line, "Hello, old friend. Remember me?"

Ciaran shook his head.

"Look, Zen, I'm in the middle of something right now. Call me back later, okay?" She hung up. Then she saw the look on Ciaran's face. "What?"

"You're quite good dealing with criminal minds." He smiled. "I'm impressed."

"It comes with the job," she muttered. They walked into the elevator and ignored the buzzing phone.

MADELINE AND CIARAN entered the grand hallway of the apartment to find a man standing there with his back to Madeline and Ciaran. He was looking out the window, down to the city.

"I thought you were in Australia," Ciaran said.

The man turned around. He was maybe an inch or so shorter than Ciaran, but they shared so many similarities that it didn't take much thought for Madeline to guess they were brothers.

"I was. I'm sorry, I didn't bring home any kangaroos or

boomerangs as souvenirs. Plus, I went back to Spain last week, and then to Rome, and so forth . . ."

"I must have lost track of your extensive travel."

The man winked at Madeline. "So as I've heard, this must be the lady, Madeline Roux!"

"I'm no lady, but you've got the name right. You're Ciaran's brother?"

"I hope he's said nice things about me."

"If you assume nothing is a nice thing," Ciaran responded. "This is Tadgh, my brother. I'm sure you could tell. Apart from some physical similarities, I don't believe we have much in common."

"Oh, come on, Ciaran. We share our parents. Isn't that enough?"

Tadgh came forward, took Madeline's hand in his, and kissed her knuckles before she could react. Then he rushed forward quickly and gave Ciaran a bear hug that took him totally by surprise.

Apparently embarrassed, Ciaran shoved Tadgh aside, saying, "Grow up."

Tadgh turned to Madeline. "I took off without saying goodbye to him, so he's a bit testy at the moment."

Madeline merely smiled.

"Mother would be very pleased to see you," Ciaran said.

"I'm sure of it. I'm her favorite. But I'd like to flop on the couch here for a couple of days before I head to Dublin. That is, if it's okay with you?"

"Don't even ask," Ciaran responded sarcastically. "Tadgh, Madeline and I have to run. But before we do, what do you want, really, apart from my couch?"

Tadgh looked at Madeline.

Ciaran said, "She's in. So you can spill it. What is it that you want?"

"In? How far in?" Tadgh asked.

"All the way in," Madeline responded. *Too fast, damn it,* she thought, judging by Ciaran's reaction—or lack thereof.

Tadgh looked at Ciaran for a confirmation, but nothing came from him. "I've heard about Robert."

"If that's your main concern, you know where they live. Pay them a visit."

"I saw a record of an entry at Mon Ciel lab." Tadgh stared at Ciaran.

"It was me. Since when do you read security reports?"

"You haven't used it for years. What could you possibly do in that rusty old lab except dig up your dead and buried problems?"

"You have no say in this. Get back to your travel extravaganza and leave the family business to those who are responsible," Ciaran snarled.

Tadgh laughed and spoke to Madeline, "You see how lucky I am to have this big brother to take care of everything!"

"Then leave if you have a problem," Ciaran growled. His migraine was coming back in waves.

Tadgh flopped onto the couch and stretched his arms out. "The thing is, Madeline, he's only good ninety-nine percent of the time. When it's time for the other one percent to take charge, he's hopeless."

Ciaran snatched Tadgh off the couch and threw him to the wall. A framed painting nearby dropped on the floor, and glass shattered everywhere.

"The computer said, *'It's time,'*" Madeline said.

"Madeline!" Ciaran growled.

Tadgh narrowed his eyes. "Say again, Madeline?"

"Madeline . . ." Ciaran objected, but his vision blurred with the headache. He strode toward the medicine cabinet to take his painkillers.

Seizing the opportunity, Madeline spilled, "The

computer in Ciaran's office turned itself on and said, *'It's time, Ciaran. Enemies are nearby.'* Ciaran said Mrs. Hanson was replaying information in her dialogue that was ten years old—without even knowing it. And she stabbed herself to frame us."

Ciaran had his eyes closed and was bracing his hands on the bench, waiting for the medication to take effect. Beads of sweat ran down his forehead. He said nothing.

"You're going back to Mon Ceil, Ciaran," Tadgh growled.

Ciaran opened his eyes. "I don't need you to tell me what to do."

"I don't know what and where Mon Ciel is, but I have a problem here. Before my friend is safe and sound, I can't go anywhere" Madeline said.

"They kidnapped her friend and used her to get to me," Ciaran said.

"Oh, I see, they've gotten smarter!" Tadgh said.

"You're saying my friend's kidnapping was just a manipulation to get to you? You knew the whole time? And my friend's life is just a pawn for someone to get in touch with your family?" Madeline waved her arms in the air, frustrated. "For what? I don't care how important your family is. Jo is everything to me. I'm done with this." Madeline turned on her heel and strode toward the door.

Ciaran darted toward her and grabbed her arm. "I didn't know at the beginning, Madeline. You have to trust me."

"You don't trust anyone. Why should I trust you?"

"My family has a lot at stake here. I understand your friend is important and I don't take her kidnapping lightly. But I do think that there is a connection between that and our family business. If you stay with me, we can work things out."

Madeline hesitated.

"You don't have anything to give Zen, and he'll be calling back any minute!"

"You're not lying to me?"

"No. And we have to go to the police station now."

Madeline nodded. Ciaran pulled Madeline into his arms and embraced her. In the background, Tadgh rolled his eyes.

CHAPTER 27

*C*iaran glanced quickly at Madeline on the passenger side of the car. She looked calm and collected. Her hand slid inside her handbag. He shook his head and reached over, gently taking the phone from her hand.

"We'll sort this out and get Jo back, Madeline."

"I know." She smiled at him, but the smile didn't quite reach her eyes.

"Thank you for your help at the police station." Ciaran tried to break the silence.

"I didn't really do anything. You had everything organized. Even if the gardener had gone to the police, he wouldn't have had a leg to stand on."

Ciaran smiled. "It's not me. Lindsay had it organized."

Madeline nodded and remained silent. She didn't seem to want to talk any further. The closer to the time Zen would call, the more Ciaran saw her wits leaving her.

He looked at the road. The business traffic was heading toward the city while they were going in the opposite direction. The traffic movement was a metaphor for his life and his family—always against the odds.

Very soon, he'd open his home to Madeline. He barely knew her, but he couldn't deny the comfort he felt when he was around her. Still, he didn't need comfort, didn't need safety, and didn't need anyone's protection. Hell, he'd let someone into his comfort zone once, and it had been a mistake he'd sworn he would never repeat.

For now, Madeline was a victim, tangled in the mess he'd created in the past. So protecting her was a mission. Happy with his reasoning, he pressed the accelerator.

The phone rang.

"Let it ring a few times," Ciaran said quickly. He veered to the side of the road and parked. Then he signaled.

He could see the screen flash on, and he cursed. He should have turned that video function off. Jo's face was pressed against the screen at first, and then she was pulled back a bit by her hair, revealing a large bruise on her forehead and a black eye. She was barely conscious.

Ciaran felt his blood boil, and he saw that Madeline had lost it. Her hands shook, her lips trembled, and tears streamed down her face. She was in no condition to negotiate.

Ciaran grabbed the phone, pointed it to the floor, and twisted it around quickly to disorient the view at the other end. Then he turned the video off.

Zen's voice came across. "Hello, sweet pea."

"Who's that?" Ciaran cleared his throat.

Zen's voice came across reluctantly. "Uhmm . . . Maddie . . . are you there?"

"She's busy. Who are you?"

"I need to talk to Madeline."

"Why?" Ciaran snapped.

"Who the fuck are you?" Zen snarled.

Ciaran cut off the call.

Zen immediately called back. Ciaran picked up, "This is our company's phone. One more harassing call to Madeline, and I'll hand you over to the police."

"Harassment? I ain't harassing anyone. She promised me something. We had a deal. If I don't get to talk to her, she'll regret it."

"Who are you?"

There was a pause. "Zen."

"Ahhh, the idiot who wanted to talk to White Knight."

"Who am I talking to?"

"Ciaran."

"Ciaran LeBlanc? Are you fucking with me?"

Ciaran cut off the phone again. Zen called back. Ciaran let it ring a few times before picking it up. "Last chance, Zen. What do you want?"

"I want to talk to White Knight."

"Talking."

"I want White Knight, the avatar in hologames."

"What part of 'I am talking' don't you understand?"

"I can't believe . . ."

"You're wasting my time. You had a deal with Madeline, not with me. If you have White Knight, what's in it for me?"

"I didn't know I'd be dealing with you. I have her little friend with me. If Madeline is with you as she claimed, then her concern should be your concern."

"That's a long shot, but go ahead."

"Well, if you *are* White Knight, then you know how to complete the other half of the program Jo developed. There is an artifact buried with John Dee. A crucifix. I want that, too. If I have those two things, then Madeline will get her little friend back."

"If that's all you want, call me back tomorrow. I'll let you know the location of John Dee's tomb."

"Why can't you tell me now?"

"I don't think a scumbag like you would honor your promises. Call me tomorrow. We'll work out a place for an exchange. We get Jo back, and you get the artifact."

"I . . ."

"You don't have a choice, Zen. As you can see, there's nothing in this for me."

"All right. I'll call you back tomorrow." Then there was the sound of a gun shot from the other end of the line. Madeline nearly passed out. She opened the car door and got out. "Hear that?" Zen taunted. "That's a real gun. Next time, I'll be aiming it at Jo's head. So don't fool around, Ciaran."

"Fuck you, Zen." Ciaran cut off the call. He opened a small compartment below the dashboard and pulled out a small box. Tipping a couple of pills onto his hand and grabbing a bottle of water, he rushed out after Madeline.

She was walking aimlessly at the shoulder of the highway. Ciaran darted forward, pulling her back and into his arms. Her body was cold, she looked at him blankly. She was going into shock. He knew the symptoms too well. She wriggled from his arms, but he was squeezing her too tight for her to break free.

"Shhhh, listen to me, Madeline. Look at me, please."

"Is Jo dead?"

"No."

"She's dead, isn't she? It's my fault."

"Don't talk. Listen to me."

"Gunshot . . . he shot her. . . I heard it . . ." She shoved Ciaran away.

He grabbed her again and shoved the pills into her mouth. He held her tight and pushed the water bottle into her mouth. "Drink this." She wriggled. "Drink, and I'll let you go." She swallowed. Then he swept her off her feet and carried her back to the car. He put her in the back seat and climbed in.

Madeline opened the car door on the other side, trying to get out. Ciaran pulled her back in and held her in his arms. After struggling for a while without success, she started to sob. Ciaran held her and rocked. And her weeping came like a storm.

Then she lay on his lap, looking up at him and grinning foolishly. "Ciaran LeBlanc." Her sultry voice was slurred with drugs. She touched his face. "Do you know how beautiful you are?"

"People don't normally refer to a man as beautiful, but I'll take that as a compliment."

She grinned. "Do you know how many men I've been with?"

"No, I don't."

"I don't have enough fingers and toes to count them."

He smiled at her as she played with his thick, dark hair.

"Do you mind?"

"Mind what?"

"That I've been with many men."

"No." He chuckled. "No, Madeline. You're a beautiful woman. It's only natural that men admire you."

She was giddy. "Got ya . . . Got ya . . ." Then her laughter slipped away. Her eyes were dreamy as she traced her fingertip across his Adam's apple, along his throat, and down his chest. "I haven't really been with that many men. I wasn't trying to be selective or anything. I've just never been drawn to anyone . . ." Her hand was on his chest now, circling, teasing. "I've never met anyone as powerful as you are."

His breath quickened and his heart skipped a beat.

"Do you know you have that power? You draw people in. Not just women. Everyone. People just love you."

"No, I don't think I have such power, Madeline."

"How many women have you been with?"

"Can you guess?"

"Many, many, many . . ." She almost sang it. Then she cupped his face in her hands. "I'd be surprised if it's not many . . ."

He looked into her big brown eyes. "Not many," he said.

She reached up and pulled him down so he lay on his back. She traced his jawline with her fingers. "You look like a dark angel, Ciaran. The moment I saw you at the park, I wanted to taste these lips." She rubbed her thumb on his lips, parting them. He bit her thumb and sucked. She yelped, delirious, and devoured his mouth with hers. Her hands traveled down his body.

He felt like he was going to explode. The blood was coursing furiously through his veins. He saw stars in his eyes. His body was tensed like a bow at a maximum stretch.

She wouldn't let go, wouldn't ease off. Her passion attacked his body without mercy. Her tenacity occupied every corner of his mind. She consumed every life force he could summon. Her energy pulsed into him like tidal waves and withdrew like a strong current.

In a very short moment, they were going to become one. They were going to invade each other's lives.

Yet he barely knew her.

He pushed her up then propped himself up, still breathing heavily. "I can't do this to you. We can't do it, here and now. You're doped up with the medicine I gave you, Madeline."

"Why not?" she murmured sleepily. He brushed the hair

back from her face and kissed her forehead as she fell asleep. Then he climbed into the driver's seat and drove her home to the mansion at Henley-on-Thames, Oxfordshire.

CHAPTER 28

The sound of the tires rolling over the gravel on the long driveway woke Madeline. She sat up in the back seat and beheld the magnificence of Mon Ciel. It was a palace—Ciaran's home. She didn't need an introduction to know where she was and what she was seeing. This place was a world in itself—separated from the outside world.

It was more than a castle, Madeline thought. This palace had the warm feeling of a home. This was the place that Ciaran called home, the place that he would not share with outsiders. But wasn't he sharing it with her by bringing her here, though? *Don't flatter yourself,* she thought. Who knew how many women had shared his bed in this palace?

She rubbed her forehead. Her head was pounding. As Ciaran stopped the car, Madeline recalled what had happened before. She stormed out of the car.

As quick as a cat, Ciaran was out of the driver's seat and after her.

"Jo?" Madeline asked.

"She's fine. Fine for now. The gun shot was just a warning. Zen didn't shoot Jo. He'll call again tomorrow." Ciaran spoke as quickly as he could.

Madeline stared at him. Then she nodded. "Oh. That's all right then. We'll have another night to prepare."

He smiled.

"Is this your home?"

Ciaran nodded. He wrapped his arm around her waist to guide her inside.

"Why was I sleeping in the back seat of the car?"

"You were tired," Ciaran explained. "The back seat is more comfortable than the front seat."

She frowned. "I remember you in the back seat as well?"

"Then who was driving?"

"Right. You're right. I must have been hallucinating. The back seat of your car is very comfortable."

"Is that so? I'll have to try it out sometime." He grinned and then yelped as she poked his side.

It surprised her that Ciaran seemed to have no live-in staff to maintain such an enormous place.

"Be careful when you walk around. There are security cameras everywhere."

She frowned and glanced around. "Where?"

Ciaran smiled. "You won't see them, but they see your every movement."

She figured that behind the antique interior made up of endless expanses of polished wood, glass, stone, and sculptures, there was an ultra-modern technology that controlled everything—from light switches to security doors.

There was not a trace of violence, death, or sorrow in this place, Madeline noticed. Unlike what Madeline had seen in other castles, towers, and even in churches, the paintings, artwork, sculptures, and tapestries in this palace did not bear a hint of blood, weapons, war, or any historical or religious activities involving blood and sacrifices.

This was a *home*.

"There are two parts of the house," Ciaran explained at they stood at the junction of two marble corridors. "The old section used to be a castle, and the new part my father added when we moved in."

"You were born here?"

He nodded and gestured toward the left wing. "In the new part of the house." Before they headed up the set of stairs, Madeline saw a group of blue dots hovering at the corridor Ciaran had referred to as the old part.

A hollow female voice echoed in the air, "Ciaran!"

Madeline turned to look toward the dots.

"Ciaran, you're home! Welcome home!" She heard the voice again from the same direction.

Noticing Madeline had stopped walking, Ciaran turned around. "There are rooms in the old wing, but they're not as nice as those in the new one."

"Did you hear that?" she asked.

"Hear what?"

Madeline looked again. The blue dots had disappeared. "Never mind," she said and followed Ciaran up the stairs.

CHAPTER 29

*M*adeline buried her bare feet in the lush carpet. She loved the softness and texture of the carpet on the soles of her feet. She smiled at the sunshine and went over to the window. In front of her was the endless lawn of the magnificent Mon Ciel. She felt like a princess in a castle. Except she wasn't waiting for a prince to climb up the tower to rescue her. Her prince was going to knock on her door any minute.

There was a knock on the door.

Ciaran stood leaning against the door frame, smiling. *The LeBlancs trademark their eyes and smiles*, Madeline thought. She had seen the same qualities in Tadgh. Striking eyes and warm smiles.

"I'm afraid I can't arrange room service," he told her. "If you want breakfast, you'll have to come downstairs with me," he said.

"All right. Let me put some clothes on." She closed the door.

As soon as she had dropped her robe to the floor, a cold wedge of air brushed over her body. Blue dots appeared in a flock. They swirled around her body, moving up and down.

Madeline froze. She heard the humming sound and the singsong voice of the woman who had called Ciaran last night.

Don't freak out. She could see people's minds, their thoughts. That meant someone with some sort of connection to her is looking at her body right now.

She put her clothes on. The flock of blue dots hovered toward a side door tucked at the corner.

"You know what, people in movies would probably follow you to their death. But I'm not that stupid. You have a good day!"

She strode to the door, opened it, and smiled at Ciaran.

"What is that?" Ciaran asked.

"What is what?"

"The brilliant smile on your face."

"Apparently I'm in a very good mood."

~

UNLIKE WHAT SHE HAD EXPECTED, the house was quiet. In fact, no one seemed to be around. In a large kitchen that opened onto a back garden, there was no breakfast waiting for them.

Ciaran turned on the coffee machine. He opened the cabinet to search for food. Sensing Madeline's confusion, he grinned. "I'd told my staff not to stock any food. But we might get lucky and find something."

Madeline nodded. "So you don't hang around here much."

"I used to. I grew up here." He pointed to a headless statue of something looking like a woman in the garden. "You can see my mark right there!"

"You beheaded the woman!"

"It was the Goddess of Kindness. I experimented with some explosive compound. I didn't know it would be such a success! My father was less than happy about it. He left the statue there to remind me of my sin."

"How old were you when you committed such a crime?"

"Very young. Way before school age. I was home schooled in my early years, and even at that age, I was reading advanced chemistry books."

So you didn't actually have a childhood, Madeline mused. *Where is his family now? Where is his father?* Madeline had the feeling Ciaran's father had passed away, but her reporter instincts told her that trying to dig for more information on that would be a deal breaker. When Ciaran was ready, he would tell her.

"That looks promising," Madeline commented, scanning a couple of boxes of something that appeared to be breakfast cereal.

Ciaran looked at the box. "Promising, indeed. And still within the use-by date!"

"Even if it was expired, I'd risk my life. I'm starving!"

"Oh, here you are! Oh, my dearest boy!" A cheery voice echoed in from the side door.

Ciaran dropped the cereal boxes on the bench and rushed toward the voice. An elderly woman with two armfuls of bags stood in the doorway.

Ciaran grabbed the bags, put them on the floor, and hugged the woman tightly, almost lifting her off the floor. "Mrs. Rutherford. It's so good to see you. You look wonderful!"

"Let me take a look at you!" She cupped Ciaran's face. "You look so pale. Doctor Thomas said you were injured. He was so right to worry about you. What have you done

to yourself? And now, you're about to eat this stale food."
Mrs. Rutherford's voice trailed off when she saw Madeline.
"You're not going to force your very pretty friend here to
have breakfast-in-a-box, are you?"

"This is Madeline Roux. She's a reporter from New
York. Boxed meals are quite normal in her line of work."

"You're making too big of an assumption, Ciaran. I have
my own chef. Ask my co-editor," Madeline corrected him.

"A reporter! You must be smart, just like—"

"Mrs. Rutherford . . ." Ciaran cut in.

"Uhmm . . ." She caught herself. "No one is going to
have any meal in any box in *my* kitchen!" Mrs. Rutherford
put the bags on the counter and started to unpack eggs,
butter, orange juice, milk, and other assorted grocery
items.

"You don't have to do this. We'll only be here very
briefly," Ciaran said.

"I have to use all the chances that I have to cook for
you! When Lindsay and the security boy told me you were
here, I was so happy, Ciaran. I don't care how short your
stay is, when you're here, you eat my food."

For a moment, Madeline saw Ciaran as a nine-year-old
boy under Mrs. Rutherford's care. She envied him, then
felt guilty about it. She distracted herself with a cup of
black coffee.

They heard the buzz of the front door and some high-
heeled footsteps.

Mrs. Rutherford looked disappointed, as if she might
not have a chance to feed Ciaran after all. Ciaran's eyes
darkened as if he knew what was coming.

"How about some orange juice to please this
old woman?"

Ciaran took the glass from Mrs. Rutherford and

drained the contents. He kissed her lightly on the cheek and then left the kitchen.

Madeline followed him. When she passed Mrs. Rutherford, the old woman murmured to her, "I can tell he likes you very much. He's never brought anyone else home since . . ."

Madeline arched an eyebrow, waiting.

"But it's not my tale to tell. He's a very good man, Madeline. He doesn't deserve to be hurt."

"Ciaran is a man with strong will. I can't protect him. But I can promise, if he gets hurt, it won't be on my account."

Mrs. Rutherford nodded.

"I envy him for having you, Mrs. Rutherford." Madeline left the kitchen.

"Madeline!" Mrs. Rutherford called from behind her.

She turned around. "Yes."

"… The LeBlancs are good people..."

"I'm not judging."

The old woman looked as if she wanted to say a lot more, but decided not to. Madeline gave her a courtesy nod and followed Ciaran.

CHAPTER 30

They exited a long hallway that led to a large reception room. A tall woman waited there. Madeline didn't need an introduction to know that she was Ciaran's mother. It wasn't just her beauty that Madeline wished she could have a fraction of when she got to that age, but her formidability.

The woman's long, dark hair was tied at the nape of her neck. Her lean, oval face was lit up with striking almond eyes, as sharp as a laser. Madeline could see that hidden somewhere in those cold eyes was the love, care, and warmth of a mother. But her affection was controlled, masked, and disguised so skillfully that had she not had years of experience in a job where she had to see through layers of lies, Madeline wouldn't have been able to see it.

"You were injured because of this girl, or so I was told?" her voice sounded like beautiful music.

"Doctor Thomas worries too much, Mother. You shouldn't have come all the way from Dublin. This is Madeline Roux. I wasn't injured *because* of her. I was injured because someone shot at me."

"You are as pretty as Tadgh described. My younger boy has exquisite taste for women. He praised your beauty."

"I don't make a living with my appearance, Mrs. LeBlanc, although it might be pleasing to people's eyes when I talk to them."

"And a smart cookie, you are! Call me Jennifer, please. I've been married to the LeBlancs my whole life, so there's no need to remind me of the association." Jennifer glanced at Ciaran.

"Please send my regards to Robert's poor family. What is your plan regarding security?"

"You don't have to worry about that, Mother. Mon Ciel should be fine."

"Is that so?" Jennifer walked toward a chair at the end of a long table and sat down, taking the most powerful position in the room. She spoke to Madeline. "My family has a lot at stake here, Madeline, just in case you wonder why we are strict with security. We know to the DNA of every staff member who ever set foot in this household." She stood up and approached Madeline. "No stranger is ever allowed in."

"Madeline is not a stranger, Mother," Ciaran growled.

"Did you scan her before she came here?"

"There was no need."

"Are you sure? Or have you just gone soft? I can see the resemblance, Ciaran."

"Resemblance of what?" Madeline asked.

"I am in charge of the family business, Mother. I can bring anyone in as I see fit."

"I don't like your tone, Ciaran."

"You wouldn't have to hear it if you stayed in Dublin."

Jennifer laughed. Her voice was like bell. "Listen to yourself, Ciaran. You sound like your father. A woman's place is in the home."

"And Father was correct."

"The protection your father built for Mon Ciel was to keep *all* of us safe. Tadgh told me you received a message about the timing. So I suggest you stay put inside Mon Ciel."

"I have things to do outside."

"You can keep her here, if it's what it takes."

"With all due respect, Jennifer, I can't stay here and be a piece of furniture. Like Ciaran, I have things to do. In fact, we have to leave now." Madeline looked at Ciaran, gesturing at her phone. Ciaran nodded.

Jennifer arched an eyebrow.

She probably isn't used to anyone talking back to her, Madeline thought.

"Very well." Jennifer sighed.

"In regard to your incidental exposure, I've gone beyond anger. I can never stay angry at you for long, Ciaran. I just wanted to see that you were safe and sound."

"Incidental exposure?"

"Oh, so you're not as totally on top of everything as you might think." Jennifer put a stack of newspapers on the table. "Don't take this family for granted, Ciaran."

"I'd never . . ." It came out in a raised voice, more like a hiss. Madeline knew it was a snap of Ciaran's control. He calmed down instantly. "I know what I have to do. It will be business as usual by the end of the week. Should I call the staff in, Mother?"

"Do as you see fit." She walked for a few steps and turned around. "One more thing, your cousin George— someone trashed his place a couple of weeks ago, looking for the artifact. He and his family were fine. Just had a bit of a fright."

Ciaran narrowed his eyes. "A couple of weeks ago? Why wasn't I informed?"

"You're not exactly on good terms with George, Ciaran. He told Tadgh. It wasn't just any artifact they were looking for. They identified the specific item."

"Is that why Tadgh came back to London?"

Jennifer smiled. "You really should talk to you brother more." Jennifer nodded a goodbye to Madeline and exited the room.

Madeline grabbed the stack of newspapers while Ciaran pulled out his cell phone and called Tadgh. He wandered over to the window, looking outside. Tadgh wasn't picking up his phone.

Madeline flicked through the pages of the paper. The two of them had made the front page of all the newspapers in the UK. Pictures of Ciaran with his arm wrapped protectively around Madeline's waist as they left the police station and when they had entered One Hyde Park were prominently displayed. All associated articles speculated about the rare public appearance of a LeBlanc at a police station in London, and about Madeline's role.

"Bloodthirsty media hounds," Madeline mumbled to herself. That's what Jennifer had meant by the unwanted exposure. The LeBlancs had never been exposed to the media.

Ciaran gave up on calling Tadgh. Madeline put the article on the table for him to see. He glanced at it.

"Robert would have never let this happen," he muttered and made himself a cup of coffee.

As she flipped randomly through the pages of the newspaper, she saw a small article on page four. "Two mysterious deaths in Mortlake." She shuffled through the other papers. On pages four and five, a series of small articles about Mrs. Hanson and Shaun the gardener. Mysterious deaths by stab wounds. No weapon found.

The exhale of breath came out of her mouth so loudly that it captured Ciaran's attention. He turned toward her, looking as if he was waiting for whatever might be coming at him next.

CHAPTER 31

"What's your family, Ciaran? Mafia?"

"I beg your pardon?"

"Anyone who goes against your family will get themselves killed," Madeline said.

"Madeline!" Ciaran's voice came out in a warning growl.

That was a pack reaction. She should have known. One of them got attacked, and the whole pack would kill to protect. She got that. She understood pack mentality. She had encountered many in her line of work. *Wolves.* Madeline could hear the word roaring in her head. Her heart pounded, and her blood pumped so hard that it felt as if her head would explode.

"Did you kill Peter?"

"Peter who?"

"The man who pulled me off the bus in front of your headquarters."

Ciaran smiled. "Ah, when we saw the news at One Hyde Park, I asked if you knew him, and you said no. You lied to me, Madeline."

"I didn't know you at that point."

"You still don't know me, Madeline. Otherwise, you wouldn't have asked me that question."

"Did you kill Shaun, the gardener?"

Ciaran shoved his hands in his pockets and stared at Madeline. "Do you really want me to answer those questions?"

Madeline stared back. *He was right.* She didn't really want him to answer because if he admitted to it, she didn't know how she could live with herself. But it his answers were no, she had revealed her distrust.

She withdrew a step and stormed out of the room.

"If you want to call a taxi, there's a phone in the hallway with a direct number," Ciaran called after her.

She raced along the corridor. She had to get out. She didn't hear Ciaran coming after her. Of course, he wouldn't. He'd shown her the door. She had questioned his family. His pack. Would she have done the same if she were in his situation?

At the front door of the house, she came to a skidding halt.

She would and could do worse.

She'd killed before. She wasn't innocent. It was a secret she'd shared with Jo, but it wasn't the reason they had built a relationship. Jo's family was hers, and she would do anything to protect them. Anything.

A short moment later, Madeline stood at the doorway. A tear trickled down her face, but she didn't bother to wipe it away. "This place does not qualify as a household in its current state."

Ciaran sat in a reading chair in the corner of the room, sipping his coffee quietly and watching Madeline over the rim. "It's waiting for the rightful and deserving owners to make it a household."

Another tear escaped Madeline's eyes. "I know you didn't do it."

"Neither did my family, Madeline. You were right—we could kill, but we wouldn't. It's not our way."

Madeline nodded. "I believe you."

She rushed in and all but fell into his arms. There, she felt his muscles quiver and his body vibrate with emotions. "Don't ever walk away from me like that again!" he said as he kissed her forehead.

"Okay, I promise. I have a temper, and sometimes, I can throw a tantrum."

"I noticed!" Ciaran chuckled. "I'll arrange a location to meet Zen and get Jo back tonight. To avoid further *misunderstanding* with law enforcement, could you liaise with your Stephen to get the police on site? If he's here."

"He's not *my* Stephen. And yes, he's here. He messaged me last night." Then she frowned. "You can do this easily with a phone call to detective Adamson, I'd imagine?"

Ciaran smiled. "Adamson is as straight as an arrow. We reported the incident at Mrs. Hanson's to him but mentioned nothing about Jo and the kidnapping, which occurred at the same time. I can go back to him with reasons for not reporting it, but regardless of how much wheeling and dealing I do, he'll suspect we have something to hide."

Madeline arched an eyebrow.

"My family doesn't deal with media and the police when it comes to our internal business. And you didn't go to the police in the first place when Jo was kidnapped—for a reason that you will one day tell me."

"Hey, I didn't call the cops because Zen threatened to . . ."

"That's the reason you'd give Stephen, but not me, Madeline."

Damn! He didn't manage a gigantic conglomerate for noth-ing. "Right, I have something to hide. But you have to admit that you need Stephen now to make arrangement with the police? Because he came here as my friend, not as a cop. He's not a big deal FBI agent or anything. He just catches small timers."

Ciaran laughed. "Madeline, don't worry. I'll be gentle with him. Okay?"

Damn, again! Am I that obvious? "Okay, I'll call Stephen," Madeline muttered and scurried out of the room.

~

TEN RINGS and Stephen had not yet picked up. Madeline walked up and down the hallway, waiting. There was no natural light although the down light was lit twenty-four/seven. The floor was covered in black stone tiles which were slightly uneven and difficult to walk on. Madeline's shoes had a bit of a heel, and they tended to slide into the gaps between the stone tiles. In addition, the hard soles of her shoes made clicks that seemed to echo through the area even though Madeline was very sure that she was walking lightly and not stomping.

Along the hallway, there were twelve white statues of what Madeline guessed must be Greek Gods. They all had kind and caring faces and looked like the sort of gods one would feel comfortable talking to—or maybe *praying* was more appropriate.

Madeline thought it a good idea to stop pacing up and down the hallway. The noise she was making might annoy those gods. Just then, one of Madeline's pointy heels got stuck in a gap between two stones. The walking momentum made Madeline fall forward, punching her palm against the toe of a god's statue. For a moment,

Madeline thought she had broken a bone in her hand or dislocated her shoulder. But no, she took a quick inventory, and she was not hurt—but the god was. The toe had broken off. She caught it before it slid off and shattered on the stone floor.

"Oh, my God! Oh, dear, sweet Jesus God, please forgive me!"

"What's that, Madeline?" Stephen's voice piped up from the other end of the line.

Madeline finished her phone call with Stephen, making an appointment to meet with him at the bakery café at the London Eyes.

She walked into the great hall, and Ciaran looked as if he was ready to go out with her to meet Stephen.

"I broke a god's toe."

Ciaran cocked an eyebrow in question.

"I broke his toe, but I'm going to fix it. All I need is some super glue."

Madeline showed him the toe in her palm.

Ciaran had a blank look, glancing at the toe and back at Madeline's expression. Then he had a fit of laughing. He looked at her standing there with a toe in her hand and thought about how much he adored her.

"Don't worry about it. I'll get someone to fix it for you!"

"No, no, it's my doing. I broke the god's toe, so I'll fix it."

Ciaran smiled. "As you like. I'm sure he won't mind having a toe missing for a few hours. But we've got to go now."

On the way out of the house, Madeline asked, "Why don't you have marble statues, or metal ones that would be sturdier and last forever? I hope these statues didn't cost a fortune."

"Nah, I bought them cheap. Just a couple of million each."

Seeing the appalled look on Madeline's face, Ciaran laughed.

"I was just kidding. The statues aren't antique or anything like that. They aren't expensive at all. That hallway connects to a new extension of the house—it was built ten years ago. The statues were added to blend the décor with the old section. The statues in the old part were all antique. I blew the head off of one of them."

"I'm sure you're the favorite child in the family!"

"That's a safe bet." Ciaran grinned.

～

IN LONDON, Ciaran swapped the car for a long black limousine. He asked Madeline to call Stephen and request that he walk across the bridge to the opposite side of the river from the London Eyes.

Before Stephen reached the car, Ciaran asked Madeline not to mention the location of his house.

A moment later, Stephen opened the limousine's door and got in. After the standard greeting, Ciaran offered Stephen some scotch. Stephen accepted and grinned at Madeline's stare.

"What? I'm not on duty."

"Please excuse this moving office. I trust you understand."

"Of course. I was surprised when you'd agreed to meet at a café." He looked at Madeline. "I'm so sorry for messing up your plan, Madeline."

"No, I appreciate your help, and I'm glad you stopped by Zen's place. It turned out to be a positive thing, actually. He thought I could play hardball."

"Could you?" Stephen asked.

"Yes, with Ciaran's help."

Stephen looked at Ciaran suspiciously.

Ciaran sipped some scotch. "Stephen, what's in this for you? I just don't believe that a normal friendship would make you travel all the way from New York to London. I don't believe in sentimental reasons, either, and am therefore assuming you have a crush on Madeline."

Stephen choked on his scotch. "Then . . . I . . . I don't have a reason."

Madeline glanced at Ciaran, warning him not be too harsh on Stephen.

"So then, what's your plan to help Madeline?"

"I'll talk to Zen and get Jo back."

"What do you have to give him?"

"Nothing. But he knows I'm a cop and I could cause him trouble."

"And you think that this is sufficient to scare Zen and get Jo back?"

Stephen looked at Madeline as if asking for a rescue.

Madeline spoke gently. "I know that London is out of your jurisdiction. But could you get some collaboration here if action is needed?"

"Depends on what kind of action. I'm on vacation. I'm not even carrying a weapon."

"So you were just being a sentimental fool, jumping on an airplane to come here without any idea what you were going to do?"

"Ciaran," Madeline warned again.

Ciaran stared at Stephen. He cocked an eyebrow and waited for Stephen to respond. Madeline knew Stephen was doing his best not to stutter under the pressure.

"Stephen, you might think that I am in no position to judge your motives or interrogate you about your actions. And you're right. You and I are in competition for the same woman, and on that ground, we are equal."

"Excuse me, do I need to get out of here?" Madeline asked, astonished.

Ciaran continued, "However, when it comes to solving the problem Madeline has at hand, I now have a stake in it more than you do. I am involved. Blood has been spilled, and I have lost a friend in the process. On top of that, I have my family and my business interests to protect. So I do hope you understand why I have to ask these hard questions."

"Yeah, yeah, sure." Stephen cleared his throat. "I understand. So what do you want me to do to help? I assume you have a plan?"

"I'm not asking you to do or give us anything. On the contrary, we're going to give you the collar."

"What?"

"We will trap Zen, and you'll catch him. Simple. But you have to make it official. You have to liaise with the cops here. How you play it out is totally up to you. I'll notify you with Zen's location when we get to it. How does that sound?"

"Ah . . . ah . . . perfect . . . I didn't expect this . . ." Stephen nodded.

"How fast can you get a team together?" Ciaran asked.

"I don't know. I've never worked with British partners before."

Ciaran pulled out a card and gave it to Stephen.

"Detective Adamson is a good man to talk to. Can you get something together soon?"

"How soon?"

"Let's say a couple of hours."

"Jesus . . ."

"Can you do it or not?"

Stephen nodded somewhat doubtfully and got out of the car.

Ciaran smiled at Madeline's astonishment.

"Two hours?" she asked.

"Well, he didn't ask for more, did he?"

Madeline shook her head and sighed. "What about your promise to me?"

"I don't think I was too harsh on him."

"He's harmless, Ciaran!"

Ciaran turned at Madeline. He rubbed his thumb on the dimple on her left cheek. "He's too good to be true, Madeline."

CHAPTER 32

*A*s soon as the screen of the video call flashed, Ciaran reached over and turned the video function off.

"Put the video on, Ciaran," Zen's voice croaked.

"You don't have anything I want to see. Do you want the location or not?" Ciaran asked.

They were sitting at a table in a private room at an exclusive restaurant in Knightsbridge. Madeline sat next to Ciaran, her eyes glued to the phone on the table, listening to his voice coming out of the speaker.

"This isn't my turf. I ain't going to fall into one your traps. I'll give *you* the location, and you bring the crucifix. I'll have equipment on site—you'll code the program for me, and then I will give you Jo."

"No. I'm not digging a grave for you. Let's meet half-way. We'll go to the tomb, and while you dig for your crucifix, I'll finish the program for you."

"And what if you set a trap for me? Call the cops or something?"

"I can do the same thing if we meet at *your* location!

Look, I don't have time to play around. I want Jo back. I don't care about the crucifix and your little program, whatever it does."

"All right . . . what's the location?"

"We'll see you tonight at seven at Rufford Abbey."

There was sound of tapping on computer keyboard. And then, "Mr. LeBlanc, you think I'm an idiot?"

"As you like!"

"Fuck you, Ciaran! That's a tourist park."

"If the tomb is at Mortlake where everyone thinks it is, do you really think whatever you want to find in it would still be there?"

Zen hesitated. "It's like three hours' drive from London . . ."

"Then you'd better start driving. Remember, you better bring Jo. Without her being safe and sound, the deal will be off. I won't give you a second chance." Ciaran hung up the phone.

When Ciaran turned to look at Madeline, her heart sank. His eyes were too dark.

"What, Ciaran?"

He gestured for silence, then dialed on his cell phone. "Lindsay, I need the chopper at the London headquarters right now. Arrange two handguns for me. Send twenty of Robert's best men to Mon Ciel. Get my mother out of there. Tie her up and drug her if you have to. I'll deal with her wrath afterward. No civilian staff in Mon Ciel tonight."

He hung up the phone, pulled out his painkiller box, and popped two pills in his mouth. Then he rubbed at his temples. Madeline pulled a chair over and sat opposite Ciaran. "Let me," she said and rubbed her thumbs on his temples. Ciaran closed his eyes, then he reached over, pulling Madeline onto his lap and nuzzling into the crook of her neck. She wrapped her arms around his shoulders and found the muscles there tightened up in knots. She pressed and kneaded them, trying to relax him.

Ciaran released her but still held on his lap. "Zen is simply too stupid to handle this by himself. Do you know what a hologame is?"

Madeline shook her head.

"It's the most advanced game technology on Earth. Jo finished only the front end of it because she doesn't have the technological resources to complete it. For Zen to say he'll arrange a computer for me on site—that suggests he knows nothing about this technology and what he's dealing with."

"You're saying that the person Zen is working for wants whatever is inside Mon Ciel?"

"I hope I'm wrong and Zen is only a stupid gold digger."

Madeline hopped up and kissed Ciaran's forehead, then grinned as she saw the twinkle return to his eyes. "What if they send more than twenty men to Mon Ciel?"

Ciaran laughed. "It's not the numbers, it's the technology we have that protects the place." He kissed her dimple. "All you need to know is that we'll get Jo back tonight, regardless of whether Zen is stupid or not. Okay?"

She nodded and got off his lap.

HALF AN HOUR LATER, Madeline and Ciaran finished the last part of the security check and headed toward a dispatch platform at the back of the building. The helicopter pilot started the engine as soon as he saw Ciaran's shadow at the door. Ciaran got into the helicopter and helped Madeline in.

Tadgh was sitting in one of the front seats, grinning at

them. "Thank you for asking Lindsay to arrange a gun for me. You know me well, brother."

"It wasn't for you," Ciaran growled.

"You weren't intending Madeline to carry, were you? Don't worry, she can handle this." Tadgh reached over and handed Madeline a gun so small that it would fit nicely into her purse, if she had one.

"Tadgh!" Ciaran warned.

"This could come in handy. Put it in your pocket. I don't think Ciaran intended to give you a weapon. He's a two-hand shooter. But he'll have to manage with one gun for tonight."

"What? Are you both combat trained?"

"No. We just bluff." Tadgh grinned again.

"If you know about tonight, then you should be at Mon Ciel," Ciaran scolded.

"No." Tadgh's grin faded. When he was serious, his eyes were as intense as Ciaran's. "Mon Ciel is only a house. *You* are my brother."

"Then don't be my burden. I don't have time to watch your ass."

"You have to. That's your responsibility." Tadgh sank deep into his chair, relaxing as if he was going to take a nap. Ciaran swallowed a snarl and asked the pilot to take off.

AT FIVE THIRTY p.m. in the winter, Rufford Abbey had already been deserted by staff and visitors. *What a magnificent sight*, Madeline thought. She was wondering how many people visited during the day. Under the very limited sunlight that was left, the abbey sat quietly as praying for the monks who had lived and died here in the twelfth century.

Once the helicopter had landed, Tadgh whined, "I hope we make it for dinner tonight."

The area was surrounded by national parks and bushland. There would be no hope for civilized comforts such as meals and accommodations in nearby locations.

"I didn't twist your arm to make you come here. We need to set up." Ciaran pointed to the parking lot. "You see that lot? We'll make the guy park there and show us clearly that he has Jo with him. Then Madeline and I will distract him and make him work to find the crucifix."

"Crucifix?" Tadgh frowned. He shot a very quick glance at Madeline, and Madeline knew he didn't realize she had caught his look. She kept her face blank, focusing on Ciaran's plan.

CHAPTER 33

*C*iaran assured Tadgh with an easy tone. "He mentioned John Dee's tomb, then an artifact, then a crucifix. I don't think he knew exactly what he was talking about."

"A gold digger you've got there." Tadgh smiled.

Ciaran nodded.

"So you want to lure him away from the car, and then we can jump in and rescue the girl?" Tadgh asked.

"That's the ideal scenario. I don't think Zen is very smart, but he might not be totally stupid, either. If he figures it out before we get to Jo, then our plan is doomed."

"You have to help us guide the cops in here to get Zen, Tadgh," Madeline said. She pulled out her phone and shared Stephen's number with Tadgh. "This is my friend, Stephen. He's a New York cop. Zen is apparently wanted by the police internationally, so Ciaran thought we might give Stephen a sexy collar on this case."

Tadgh shook Ciaran's shoulders. "Nice!"

Then they went about setting up the venue while

Madeline followed up with Stephen on his progress. Everything seemed to be going as planned.

Just after seven, a car drove slowly into the dark parking lot. As soon as the headlights went off, Madeline's phone buzzed, and Zen's voice was broadcast on speaker.

"Well, we're here. Got lost a bit but didn't kill myself by driving on the wrong side of the road."

"Where's Jo?" Madeline asked.

Zen switched on the internal light of the car. Jo was leaning back, sleeping in the back seat of the car.

Tadgh gasped. "Oh, sweet Jesus Christ, what a sleeping beauty!"

Both Madeline and Ciaran turned around, their eyes commanding silence. He made an apologetic zipping gesture across his lips and shut up.

"I had to give her a sedative. She wasn't exactly cooperating, as you might realize, Madeline. She should wake up in a couple of hours. So what's next?"

Ciaran leaned toward the phone while he signaled to Tadgh to go away. "All right, we're in the main abbey. I'll meet you at the door."

Five minutes later, Zen appeared at the entrance to the abbey. Madeline and Ciaran met him at a stone door to the side. The door was small, and Ciaran had to bend down to go past it. Zen followed and then Madeline. Madeline checked behind her before entering the chapel area and caught a flash of Tadgh's shadow running between the trees. She smiled to herself. Just like his brother, he was as quick as a cat.

The chapel was made entirely of stone, and thus it was freezing. Some burning torches mounted on the walls dimly lit the interior, and it was just enough to give light and keep the ambience of the old place of worship. An old altar, consisting of a non-operating platform that looked as if it was now used as a fireplace, was located at the far end of the room. Paintings and information about the history of the abbey covered part of the cold stone walls.

Along with the noise of birds and wild animals from the nearby lake and bushland, the quivering shadows and the feeling in the air inside the abbey caused a chill to run up Madeline's spine. If anyone had told her that the ghost of an ancient monk haunted this place, she would have believed it. Madeline admired Ciaran for choosing such a place for their setup. Still, Madeline wished she wasn't standing in one of King Henry VIII's ruined abbeys. Surely some of the ghostly things people talked about occurring in these dark and mysterious abbeys were real.

"What the hell is this?" Zen broke the silence.

"This is where the crucifix is possibly buried," Ciaran answered.

"How could the tomb possibly be in here?"

"You confuse me, Zen." Ciaran spoke sternly.

"What?"

"First you said crucifix, but now you say tomb." Ciaran shoved his hands into his pockets as if annoyed.

"Don't fuck around with me."

"Although I'm not religious, I would expect that it's disrespectful to swear at a place of worship. But given you're going to dig around, I suppose that's much worse than swearing, so I'll save my comments. Now, please clarify for me . . . do you want to dig up a tomb? Or do you want to find a crucifix?"

"Are you trying to mess with my head? I want the crucifix, of course. Why would I want to dig up a grave?"

"I certainly wouldn't want to," Ciaran muttered.

Madeline waited for a buzz on her phone—the agreed-upon signal of good news from Tadgh. There was nothing.

"There are two possible locations of the crucifix—one

is here, and the other one is in the ruined compartment around the corner. That part has not been restored, thus there is no light of any sort inside. I thought you might want to dig in here first, as it's warm and cozy."

"Dig? I thought you said no tomb digging?"

"No, I said no *tomb*. I didn't say anything about no digging."

Madeline felt as if her head was about to burst. *Tadgh, Tadgh, Tadgh!!! What is he doing? What about Stephen? Where is he? How long can Ciaran drag this out?*

"What the fuck are you doing? You really want to mess me up?" Zen's face started to turn red.

"I want to get out of here more than you do, Zen. If you want your reward, you're going to have to work for it. You want the crucifix? Then you've got to dig," Ciaran stated firmly.

"I won't do any digging. *You'll* have to dig." Zen threw a tantrum.

Ciaran smiled. "It's bad luck to disturb spirits in a place like this. So no, I won't be doing any digging."

The phone in Madeline's pocket buzzed. At the same time, a car alarm sang loudly from the distance.

"I knew it! I fucking knew it!" Zen screamed and rushed outside the room. Ciaran stopped him with a kick. Zen rolled over, falling back inside the abbey. Ciaran pulled his gun and pointed it at Zen.

On the ground, Zen grabbed a wooden bow, an exhibit item next to a statue of a monk praying, and blasted dust at Ciaran's face. He followed with a kick to Ciaran's gun, and before Ciaran knew it, Zen swung a displayed scepter at Ciaran's head. Ciaran dropped to the floor. Madeline pulled her little gun out, and at the same time, Zen pulled his gun.

They stood facing each other, at point blank range.

Saying nothing, Madeline pulled the trigger, aiming straight at Zen. Zen did the same thing. Ciaran pulled at Madeline from the ground, and she fell over and out of the bullet's range. The bullet put a large ding on the wall behind her.

Zen took the opportunity to run from of the chapel. Then from the outside, Zen kicked the heavy oak door closed and jammed the outside with some wood logs.

"Goddamn it!" Ciaran kicked at the door although he knew it wouldn't help. Madeline tried to call Tadgh, but the signal wouldn't pierce the thick stone walls.

There was a display table showing visitors how the abbey was built and the process used to make the stone walls. Ciaran grabbed the steel hammer from the display and used it to hit at the door handle until the wood logs on the outside gave way.

Cold wind slapped at their faces when they ran outside. "This way." Ciaran pointed toward the bush.

Madeline didn't know where the light was coming from, but she could see the shadows of weird-looking tree branches reaching out across the ground from the darkness, twining together as if they were holding hands to create an evil web in which to ensnare them. She kept running and trying to work the phone at the same time.

They could see Zen stumbling in the bushes. Madeline heard water splashing against the shore. The unmistakable sound of water, a lot of it. Then she remembered—there was a lake, a very large one, and there might be some swampy areas.

They seemed to be walking along a small bridge. It was really dark. Something that looked like an enormous bat flew at her. Madeline yelped and lost her balance, but Ciaran caught her.

Zen's turned. He saw them. He spun around again, then

stumbled over something and fell. He stood up quickly and ran.

In another direction, they could see Tadgh approaching. He sprinted quickly in the dark. Madeline didn't think Tadgh saw them, but he certainly caught sight of Zen. He charged toward him.

Ciaran took off as fast as he could. Madeline couldn't keep up.

Then there was another set of footsteps, loud and clear. Madeline looked around, but she couldn't see who it was.

Ciaran had disappeared into the darkness. She had to follow him. She kept running.

She was soon catching up with Ciaran and could see him approaching Zen from behind. Tadgh was running straight toward Zen. It was so dark. The shadows kept switching on and off and jumping around from the dim light shining down from somewhere in the sky. It felt as if there was moonlight, but it was too hard to tell.

Tadgh just realized he was running straight for Zen when Zen raised his gun. It was too late for Tadgh. There wasn't much he could do. It was too dark to seek something to hide behind. The only thing around Tadgh was shadow filled with thin, chilly air. For a moment, looking straight at the gun muzzle, Tadgh could feel the brush of death.

A gunshot echoed in the air.

Zen's body slumped down to the cold mud, his gun still in his hand. Tadgh could see Ciaran standing tall behind Zen's body.

Ciaran had shot Zen.

Madeline approached from behind Ciaran, and then from the side, Stephen appeared. Stephen saw Ciaran holding the gun. The scent of gunpowder still hovered in the air. Stephen approached, holding his hand out for Ciaran's gun.

"He would have shot Tadgh if Ciaran hadn't shot him first." Madeline cried, grabbing Stephen's arm. Stephen shrugged her hands off. This was the first time since they had known each other that Stephen had acted like this.

"Ciaran's a civilian. He has no right to execute another man, criminal or not. And it *wasn't* in self-defense," Stephen stated clearly.

Ciaran said nothing. He gave Stephen his gun.

"No, no . . ." Tadgh charged forward as if he was going to take Stephen down.

Ciaran grabbed Tadgh, stopping him from attacking Stephen.

"Jo." Ciaran snapped back to reality and ran back to the car.

CHAPTER 34

*T*he car park was dark. The air was deadly quiet. Ciaran ran, and in front of him was one vision—Jo lying in the car, dead. It was too dark to tell, and much too quiet for his liking. The others were calling him from far back, but he ignored them. If anything had happened to Jo, it would be his fault.

He had severely underestimated Zen. Sometimes his arrogance was his worst enemy. He'd had no right to assume that Zen was stupid.

The car stood lonely in the car park.

He reached the car before Madeline and opened the car door. It was totally empty.

Stephen approached and shined a light into the car.

"The car is empty, Ciaran. Jo isn't here," Stephen said.

"But we saw her!" Madeline asked.

Ciaran looked at the car floor. He saw a box that looked like a mini projector. "Oh, fuck me . . . it was a fucking hologram!" Ciaran grunted out the words in frustration. He kicked the car. He could feel his blood boiling, and soon his rage would come. He turned around, looking for

Madeline. For the first time in his life, during a chaotic moment when he was confused and afraid of his own rage, he needed to hold on to her.

She was his constant.

Before he could say anything, and before the rage he was afraid of flooded his mind like tidal waves, Madeline interlaced the small delicate fingers of her hand with his. Warm. Steady. And she just looked at him. And somehow, he just knew his rage wouldn't surface this time.

From the far end of the car park, the deep voice of Detective Adamson yelled, "I'm calling the crew back. We should wrap up here."

Stephen, Madeline, and Ciaran walked toward Adamson. The detective continued. "What's with Zen? Bullet in the head!"

Stephen looked at Ciaran. Madeline looked at Stephen. Ciaran said nothing.

Stephen's eyes paused on Ciaran's face for a moment, and then he pulled Ciaran's gun out. Stephen said calmly, "I announced myself and asked the offender to put his weapon down. He was aiming at Ciaran. Then he swung the gun at me. So I had to get the gun off him. We struggled. Then Ciaran jumped in, and the gun went off. Apparently, Zen took the stray bullet. I followed protocol, detective."

Adamson nodded. "I need the report in writing."

Stephen nodded.

As Adamson gathered his team together, Ciaran approached Stephen. "Thank you. I owe you one."

"Was the gun registered under your name?" Stephen asked.

Ciaran shook his head, and Stephen nodded.

Madeline approached and looked at Stephen with appreciation.

Ciaran glanced around, looking for his brother, and saw Tadgh approaching the car. He could see a small dot of red light flashing from under the car, close to the rear wheel.

"Tadgh, the car is rigged," Ciaran screamed.

Tadgh turned and ran from the car. But it seemed he was too late. The car exploded. The loud explosion tore through the quiet air. Birds darted out from their sleeping nests, and wild animals leaped from nearby bushes. The car was in flames. Fire shot out from it in waves.

Tadgh's body was thrown in the air and landed with a thud in the cold grass.

Ciaran darted toward him. That was his stubborn brother lying in the mud, the one he promised his father he would look after.

"Come on, bastard, breathe! Answer me! Open your eyes! Come on!" Ciaran thrust the phone toward Madeline, saying, "Call Doctor Thomas."

He took Tadgh's pulse. "Come on, come on! Keep breathing!" Then he shook Tadgh's shoulders. "Open your eyes and look at me!"

No response.

"Open your eyes, for fuck's sake!". Ciaran peeled off his coat and jacket quickly, leaving himself with only a white business shirt. He rolled his jacket and tucked it under his brother's head to stabilize his neck. Then he covered Tadgh with his coat.

"Now that you're warm and comfortable, open your eyes and look at your brother!"

Doctor Thomas and Lindsay arrived in the helicopter.

"He landed badly, but I think his neck is fine," Ciaran said to Doctor Thomas. The doctor did a quick visual check and cleared Tadgh to be airlifted. Madeline jumped on the helicopter with Ciaran.

Before taking off, Madeline looked at Stephen, miming her thanks. Stephen nodded and smiled. Madeline saw the gentle look in his soft green eyes, and at that moment, she understood why she hadn't given him a chance before—he was too good for her.

The helicopter went straight to Ciaran's house at Hanley-on-Thames. A large section of the new quarter had been lit up in anticipation of their arrival. After passing through layers and layers of doors, Tadgh was finally pushed inside a room that looked like an operating room.

"Why not bring him to the hospital, Ciaran?" Madeline asked.

"We have the best equipment here, and Doctor Thomas is one of the best surgeons in the country. Please wait here," Ciaran said to Madeline. "And you, too." Then he disappeared into the operation room.

At that moment, Madeline realized she was standing next to Ciaran's mother, and that he had just told his mother to wait outside the operating room.

THE LONGER MADELINE STOOD WAITING, the more her brain went numb. For the entire trip in the helicopter, Ciaran's universe had revolved around Tadgh. He hadn't responded to her questions. He didn't hear her at all. She could see the emotion blasting at him, even bigger than the bomb that had blasted at Tadgh. The scene of Ciaran kneeling next to Tadgh's lifeless body kept replaying in her head. He looked as if his own life depended upon Tadgh's survival—so much so that she dare not ask any *what if* questions. He hadn't touched her at all during the trip home. Not a hold of the hand. Not a single look. He was completely alone in his grief and concern for his brother. And so was she.

Where was Jo?

Was she okay?

Had she escaped?

Will Tadgh be okay?

Madeline shuddered in the chill air. Maybe there was an open window somewhere causing this cold atmosphere. She was standing in the corridor with the god statues, one of them still with a missing toe. She must have made them angry.

The blue dots appeared again, gathered in the corner. If she wasn't mistaken, they were dancing at her despair.

Then she looked at Ciaran's mother and realized that the chill she felt was not from an open window—it was from Jennifer. The woman could shatter her bones just by her stare.

She approached Madeline slowly, like a snow leopard observing its wounded prey before cutting its life short. With a calm voice, she stated, "You brought my older son a bullet. Now you brought my younger one a bomb. What will you bring next to this family, Ms. Roux?"

It was weird to hear her last name spoken in that way. She gave it an emphasis, an accent that brought a totally different meaning to the ordinary word. Her last name. His family. Disaster after disaster. She was going from bad to worse. It was she who had brought bad luck. It was her responsibility.

It was because of what she had done in the past.

It was her fault.

Madeline looked at the door to the operating room. It had been a while. The door was still closed. "Can I stay to make sure that Tadgh is okay?" she asked.

"No. My son, my worries. You've done enough harm. Let us live in peace!"

She was right. Madeline had no place here, in this magnificent palace.

She had to find Jo.

Madeline stormed out of the room, walking down the hallway with the line of statues.

CHAPTER 35

*B*efore she knew it, Madeline was outside the high stone walls of the estate. The steel door shut behind her, and the darkness opened in front of her.

Madeline walked. She was chilled-to-the-bone cold. She should call a taxi. She pulled out her phone and found herself dialing Stephen's number. The only number in her address book. The only person she could call for help.

She walked along a main road outside the estate. It was a tree-lined street, but she wasn't sure it could be called a road. If she called a taxi, she wouldn't even know where to ask them pick her up. Madeline realized that she was in the middle of nowhere.

She wondered how Stephen could find her. She turned on the Internet to search for maps. She needed to navigate for herself. She was close to a national park and was indeed in the middle of nowhere. She kept walking. Her teeth started to chatter. The cold air crept through her clothes and brushed her skin. She realized that she had left her beloved red leather jacket at Mon Ciel.

And then she heard the jingles—those from Mrs. Hanson's earrings. But the old woman was dead, Madeline reminded herself. She looked around. The Roman soldiers on Fosse Way had had bells that made the same noise. But she saw no one. Nothing but darkness. She was sure she was awake.

"Roman soldiers, my ass," she cursed.

The cold air started cutting into her flesh, so she walked faster. Before she realized it, she was galloping down the road. The ground seemed to slope downward. She was going down a hill, but she wasn't sure she was following a path. It was much too dark to see.

In the distance, she saw a flash of car headlights. That had to be Stephen. It had to be. The light was so dim and far away. It was so small that Madeline felt as if she was running through an endless tunnel, and the light was always just out of reach at the end. It might take her a lifetime to get there.

She called Stephen. "I think I can see you. I can see your car headlights."

Stephen turned on his speaker and held the phone in one hand while he steered the car using the other. "I can't see you, Madeline. I can't see anything. It's too dark. I guess I'm driving toward you if you can see my headlights. I'll blink. Okay? Tell me if you can see it."

Stephen switched the headlights on and off three times.

"Yes, I can see it. From a very long distance, though. Keep on the road. I know it's hard to see."

"Tell me about it!"

Madeline yelped and dropped her phone on the ground. A searing pain had cut through her right arm. She grabbed at it. She couldn't see, but she could feel what she knew was warm blood running out from what felt like a gash. She heard the sound of something hitting a tree trunk right next to her. From her experience at Fosse Way, Madeline knew it was a gunshot.

She grabbed the phone she'd dropped on the ground. It was still working, and Stephen's voice was coming out from it. "Madeline? Madeline, what happened? Did you fall?"

"I was shot," she said.

Madeline ran toward Stephen's headlights. She could see the lights moving a lot more quickly, as if Stephen had accelerated.

One more shot missed her and went past. She could hear footsteps in the mud and shallow water behind her. She couldn't tell how many people were chasing her. "I think they shot at the LED light of the phone. I have to turn it off."

"Don't. I can't find you if you turn it off."

"Bluetooth is on," she said and slipped the phone into her back pocket, running for her life.

Without the light on the phone, the bullets missed her widely. But Madeline knew she wouldn't be able to keep on like this for long. If they sprayed, that would be the end of her. She dodged and zigzagged as much as possible. She felt dizzy. She must be bleeding badly.

Stephen's headlights got closer and closer, and she could hear the car engine. Madeline ran straight toward the light.

She heard a grunt and saw a shadow flying at her, tackling her. She fell, sliding on slippery grass and rocks.

The shadow howled. It had to be chimpanzee, she thought, by the shape of it. It tried to strangle her. She heard more footsteps. Maybe from those with guns. Madeline knew if she couldn't get rid of this monkey, she was doomed. She grabbed a rock near her hand and gave a hard blow to the head of the chimp. It roared and slapped at her so hard that she thought her neck would snap. Madeline flipped and pushed the chimp aside.

Stephen's car stopped right in front of her. Its headlights shone straight onto the creature—a tall, bearded, strange-looking man who was grabbing his head. His eye was bleeding severely. Madeline must have taken his eye out with the rock. He stood up, growled, and fled into the bush. She could hear the other footsteps running away.

Stephen jumped out of the car and charged toward Madeline. "Are you hit again?" he asked.

"No," she replied and helped her into the car. The he turned around and drove away quickly.

It was nearly dawn, but the winter sun was in no way near to giving them any sign of daylight. The car's headlights showed just enough of the road ahead so that they didn't veer off into the bushes. They hadn't driven far before an extreme flash of light beamed at them from ahead. An engine roared loudly, and a truck charged straight at their pitiful rented car. From the shape, the sound, and the speed of the truck, Madeline knew they were no competition.

The truck hit their car head on. One hit, and their headlights were gone. A second hit and the hood of their car gave in, the engine hissed, and the windows cracked.

Stephen backed the car away quickly. He tried to keep it straight, but the road they were driving on was not exactly straight. Madeline knew their car couldn't handle another hit. Stephen kept reversing the car quickly. They slid off the road and flew through the air. The car landed on the fast-running creek.

"Get out." Stephen pulled Madeline out of the car. They

held on to each other, trying to stay afloat and letting the water carry them downstream.

Madeline saw the crack of dawn before her world went black.

CHAPTER 36

*D*octor Thomas turned off the operation light, pulled his medical mask off, and smiled. Ciaran released a sigh of relief. He had the same medical knowledge as Doctor Thomas did, so the doctor didn't bother explain to Ciaran about Tadgh's condition. "Well, I don't think he'd need to be sedated any longer. I'll give him some painkillers when he's up," the doctor said.

"Lucky bastard," Ciaran muttered and grinned. He pulled out his cell phone and turned it on when he saw a message from Detective Adamson flashing. He didn't check the message but called straight back.

"Adamson," the greeting was brusque and almost grumpy. Then Ciaran noticed the time—it was five in the morning.

"I apologize, Detective. I lost track of time."

Adamson snorted. "That's all right. Doctors and cops don't work by the clock. I've got good news for you. On the way back from Rufford Abbey, I got a call. Turns out Jo ran to a police station and reported the kidnapping. She put down your name as the contact person. Very smart girl. Because of the case at Mortlake, your name is in my file and high priority, so the station tagged me."

"Is she all right? Where is she now?"

"She's fine and at the station. I'll call you back later to confirm the status. Is that okay?"

"That's perfect. Thank you very much, Detective. I'll give Madeline the good news."

Ciaran hung up the phone and walked a couple of steps when it hit him—tidal waves of pain in his brain. He grunted, doubled over, and grabbed his head. Doctor Thomas darted over.

Ciaran couldn't hear anything except a robotic voice from a hollow distance, "It's time, Ciaran. The enemies are coming." The pain was excruciating, and blood trickled from his nose. All the monitors in the room flashed, and text came across all of them—"It's time, Ciaran. The enemies are coming." Doctor Thomas helped Ciaran to stand. Ciaran stood to his full height, towering over the doctor, then slumped to the floor and blacked out.

He awoke, lying on the floor, with Doctor Thomas crouched next to him. "How long was I out?" he asked.

"About thirty seconds. How often does this happen, Ciaran?"

Ciaran sat up. "It was thirty-*three* seconds that I blacked out, wasn't it?"

Doctor Thomas glanced at his watch. "Perhaps. What does that mean, Ciaran?"

Ciaran stood up, leaning on a bench for a moment to regain his balance. "A long time ago when I was developing a computer program, I came across a cross-over point between alchemy, astrology, and string theory."

"String theory? As in the context of parallel universes?"

Ciaran nodded.

"It's a very strange logic to combine these areas together! Like marrying a horse to a kitten."

Ciaran winced. "Well, it would definitely require creativity when it comes to their physical incompatibility. But anyway, my strange combination of theories suggested that a major galactic event would occur every thirty three years, where exchanges would be made between universes."

"What sort of exchanges?"

"Energy. Power. Before Father died, he told me that a man has to live up to his duty. But if I ever decided against my duty, he would understand. Then he told me to pay attention to thirty-three. I didn't know what he meant. But in the last two weeks, with all the migraines and strange static occurrences on computers, I think it has something to do with the theory." Ciaran shrugged. "Thirty-three has some theological meaning. But thirty-three what? Months? Days? Seconds?"

Doctor Thomas approached Ciaran and looked straight into his eyes. "It's thirty three *years*, Ciaran. It has been exactly that many years since you blew up the head of the Goddess of Kindness."

"It was only a statue."

"Yes, but it was the first time your trait of violence surfaced, Ciaran. Your father consulted me on that. I told him it was a violent trait, but he believed otherwise. He called it demon."

Ciaran shook his head. "It's Daimon, not demon, Doctor Thomas. The first is philosophical, and the second is theological."

"Philosophy of what?"

"A virtuous life," Ciaran headed toward the door. "Please don't tell my mother anything until I figure this out."

~

A BLAST of cold air greeted Ciaran when he walked out of the operation room. Jennifer rushed over from a corner.

"Tadgh is fine, Mother. He has some internal bleeding, but he's fine now. He'll be up and running around in no time," he said and saw some relief on his mother's face. He knew he had worried her, and he regretted that. He wanted to embrace her, but then he thought better of it and let the thought pass.

Tadgh would have dived right in, hugging and kissing his mother without any hesitance, not giving a flying thought to who might be watching him. His brother had a warm personality that Ciaran liked, but he would never admit it. That was his problem. He'd never admitted his emotions. Ciaran could count exactly the handful of occasions in his life when he'd embraced his mother.

Then he glanced around. It wasn't the cold breeze that had blasted him, it was the emptiness of the space.

"Where's Madeline?" he asked.

Jennifer stopped on the way into the operation room. "She left." She turned to proceed into the operating room, but Ciaran darted forward, blocking her way.

"What did you say to her?" His voice was so low that it was hardly audible. But he knew his mother had heard him well enough.

"Nothing. She just left."

"Even when she wasn't sure if I was a murderer, she came back to me. She stayed with me during my rage, Mother! What did you say to make her leave me?"

"I reminded her that she brought you a bullet and Tadgh a bomb. I just asked her what she would bring us next."

Ciaran withdrew a step because he wasn't sure of the consequences if he didn't.

"Don't look at me like that, Ciaran!"

He turned around and strode down the hall. He heard his mother asking from behind, "Which part of what I said to her wasn't true?"

Ciaran galloped up the stairs to his office and stormed into the control room. He activated the control panel with one hand, and with the other hand he flipped the telecom on and called his security.

On the control panel, a large round circle appeared. He coded in and activated the chip in Madeline's cell phone. His hands shook a bit as he finished. He stared at the screen. Within seconds, a small, green blinking dot appeared. The round circle on the screen spun like a compass, and the location of the green dot appeared on the screen. Ciaran transferred the data to a portable device and hurried down the stairs to the front where his men had the helicopter ready for him.

The creek was cold at dawn. The natural light was just enough for Ciaran to see Madeline and Stephen hanging on to a rock in the middle of the fast-moving water. He wanted to go down there to lift Madeline up. He wanted to touch her, to feel that she was alive. But he knew better.

He stood aside and let the rescue team go down to the creek with their stretchers. As soon as they had loaded her onto the helicopter, he grabbed her wrist to check for a pulse and was almost giddy when he found it was strong and steady.

She was a hell of a fighter when it came to survival. Ciaran checked Stephen and found the same strong, steady pulse. Neither were conscious, and the fact they'd clung to the rock in the freezing water amazed Ciaran. He took them home.

$\mathcal{A}$n hour seemed like an eternity to Ciaran. Finally, he saw Madeline open her eyes. It amazed him that he had been able to totally control his emotional reactions—the urge to hold her in his arms, to hear her heartbeat, and to feel the vibration of her emotions inside that delicate body assaulted him without mercy and left him defenceless.

He rushed to the bed, pulled her up, and let her body melt into his arms.

Then he released her and said, "Yesterday you promised me you wouldn't walk away from me."

"I might have to break that promise. I only bring you disaster, Ciaran. Nothing good is going to come from you staying with me."

"If you come with a package, I'll take all of it. Why don't you give us a chance?"

She shook her head. "I have to find Jo."

"If we find Jo, will you stay with me, or will you go back to New York?" The question came as a surprise to her, and to him as well. Madeline gave no answer.

"Is Stephen okay?" she asked.

"Yes. Doctor Thomas has taken care of him. He had some minor external injuries. But he's fine. He'd already told me about the attack from his end. He didn't know what happened before he got to you."

"Just after I left Mon Ciel, they attacked me. I don't know how many of them were there—or who they were. I think it was the same people who attacked me at Fosse Way. They shot at me again." She looked down to her injured arm, and frowned.

"You don't feel any pain now because of the painkillers. We make the best." He smiled and sat on the side of her bed. "Madeline, I have a very complicated family."

"Tell me about it!"

"After we find Jo, and if you decide to stay, I'll tell you what you want to know."

His phone buzzed.

"We have to find Jo first," Madeline said emphatically.

Ciaran looked up from his phone and grinned. On the computer screen, Jo looked at Madeline with a big, bright smile on her face. Her catlike, green eyes glittered, and her long black hair was pulled back in a ponytail. "Madeline!" Jo yelped in joy.

Madeline was speechless, and tears flowed.

"Come on, Madeline, don't do that. I'm good now. I could do a somersault right now, but I don't think it's very ladylike to do so, and I might frighten Mr. Serious Detective here." Jo turned aside and winked at him. "I need to cheer her up."

"Keep talking, Jo," Madeline said.

"I got really lucky. In the afternoon, after Zen talked to you, a couple—I don't even know their names—broke into the hotel. They beat Zen up pretty bad and let me go."

Madeline smiled but her tears kept falling.

"The couple told me to hide for a bit before going to the police. So I did. I went to the police early in the evening. Then late that night, Detective Adamson contacted the station and picked me up. I'm in his office right now."

"Last night, I thought—"

"I know. Michael— Detective Adamson told me. It must have been hard on you and everyone involved. I'm so sorry. But I'm fine now. When we finish with the paperwork here, he's going to take me right over to your place . . ." Jo turned sideways. "What? You don't know where she is?"

Ciaran walked over and hopped onto the bed. "Jo, I'll send someone to pick you up."

Jo stared at the screen and cooed, "You must be Ciaran. Thank you for everything you've done for me."

"I didn't do a thing. You saved yourself, Jo. And it was a very smart move to name me as your contact person. You know how to pull strings."

Jo grinned. "You set the strings up first. Otherwise, I'd have had nothing to pull."

"Have you been to England before?"

"Haven't had the pleasure."

"Why don't you stay for a few days? There are many wonderful places to see."

"You made my dreams come true, Ciaran." Jo beamed at the screen. "Madeline and I can finally do our girl shopping in London!"

Madeline nodded. They heard Detective Adamson calling out for Jo. She rolled her eyes. "Paperwork. See you soon. Love you both." She grinned at Madeline and Ciaran and disconnected the call.

"Inviting Jo to stay . . . Very clever, Ciaran. Thank you." She smiled and linked her fingers with his.

As soon as she touched him, he felt the comfort he'd

been longing for. Not the comfort, perhaps, but the fear of having it and then losing it—the fear of what came afterward. Something wasn't right. Ciaran shook the thoughts out of his mind.

"Hungry?" he asked.

"Famished."

"Then let's fix that."

Ciaran and Madeline left the room and found Tadgh standing in the hallway, leaning against the opposite wall with a big grin on his face.

"What are you doing up here?" Ciaran asked.

"Rumor has it that our princess was up, so I just wanted to come to say hello."

Madeline smiled, approaching to give Tadgh a kiss. "How are you, Tadgh?"

"Better than you were at dawn. You scared the hell out of my big brother." Tadgh paused, making a humming noise, then pressed on. "You're still mad at Mother, aren't you?" he said to Ciaran. "Come on, she doesn't deserve your wrath. Be mad at me. You can punch me, if you like."

"Grow up, Tadgh."

"This is as grown up as I can be at the moment. Give me a few more years, will you?"

"Take your time. Mrs. Rutherford is in, and I'm going to introduce Madeline to her famous jam and scones." Ciaran slid his arm around Madeline's back to lead her down the hallway.

"Ah . . ." Tadgh mumbled something.

"What?" Ciaran asked, without turning back.

"Mum is waiting for you in the Great Reception."

Ciaran slowly turned around as if accepting a challenge. "Very well. Would you accompany Madeline to the kitchen?"

"Ah . . . mum asked for *both* of you, actually."

Ciaran knew what was coming and opened his mouth with the intention of asking Madeline to go to the kitchen to stay out of this, but she had already grabbed his arm. "Come on. Let's go have a chat with her."

He had no choice but take her with him. Tadgh followed without making a sound.

CHAPTER 38

*T*he Great Reception room was used for family gatherings. Jennifer remembered vividly Conan sitting in the chair in front of the fireplace. Her husband had loved to watch her teach baby Tadgh to walk—he fell so many times trying to run. Conan had gotten a thrill out of a young Ciaran presenting him with new chemical formulas that he had mixed from his mother's cooking recipes.

Ciaran had been only four turning five, but he'd been able to heal many injured wild animals he found in their yard by using things he found in the kitchen and the garden. That pleased Conan tremendously, inasmuch as he was devastated when Ciaran mixed his first explosive compound and blew up the head of the Goddess of Kindness statue. Conan had then put the statue in the middle of the yard to remind Ciaran of the consequences of violence. But Jennifer knew that wouldn't work for Ciaran.

She knew her son.

And she would do whatever it took to keep him safe and to keep this family together under the roof of Mon

Ciel. They couldn't afford mistakes this year. She couldn't allow strangers in the house this year.

She knew what was behind the number thirty-three. But she would take the secret to her grave. Revealing it to Ciaran would undo his life. She would rather rot in Hell than doing that.

So for now, she had to eliminate the immediate threat —those strangers in their home—and she had to live with Ciaran's resultant wrath.

Ciaran and Madeline walked in, followed by Tadgh.

Jennifer sat on a chair at the top of a long dining table. "I'm sorry about what happened to you last night, Madeline," she spoke gently.

"They couldn't get to me last night, whoever they were, but I'm sure they'll find another opportunity."

"You're a reasonable girl, Madeline. I'm sure you won't mind me arranging a late breakfast here. I feel like a morning tea myself. Then we can discuss some family business."

"Your house, your rules, Jennifer."

"That's a good sign. We're starting to understand each other a bit better now. Why don't you all sit down?"

Tadgh didn't need a second invitation. He grabbed a chair and settled in.

"Tadgh travels extensively and has experienced great foods all over the world, but he always craves Mrs. Rutherford's scones and jam. At one point, he asked me to express post them to him when he was in Africa!" Jennifer smiled.

"Mother, that's not to be spread around. You promised me," Tadgh protested.

"You were lucky you didn't ask *me* to do that." Ciaran smiled slightly.

"That wasn't luck. I was being smart."

"You know, Madeline, Ciaran's father called this place

'Mon Ciel,' as if this was his blue sky, his heaven, his world. And he wasn't talking about the palace. He meant the family that he loved with all of his heart. Am I correct, Ciaran?"

"What are you getting at, Mother?" Ciaran lowered his voice.

"The LeBlancs were blessed with their fortune, but they were also cursed with secrets, Madeline," Jennifer said.

"She doesn't need to know any of that," Ciaran growled out in protest.

"As you can see, like his father, my son will do whatever it takes to protect the family secrets . . ."

"Mother!" Ciaran stood up.

"And as you can see, he was about to bully his mother out of her place."

"I would never—"

"Then you will give me a fair chance to speak to Madeline. I think she cares for you, so she should hear what I have to say. Don't you agree, Madeline?"

Madeline nodded. "I'll listen, but I'll reserve judgment. There's nothing you can do or say to influence me."

"Naturally! And Ciaran, I will only speak the truth, and if you think otherwise, you can have your say. Of course, that will only happen if you stay. Would you rather stay or leave the room, Ciaran?"

Ciaran sat down slowly, giving Jennifer a warning look.

Jennifer smiled. "Yes, I'd rather you stay. Madeline, Ciaran loved his father—no, more precisely, he worshipped his father. Before you object, Ciaran, let's say you loved your father very much. Is that better?"

No response from Ciaran.

"Yes or no, Ciaran?"

"Yes, I loved Father," Ciaran snarled.

"So much so that your world seemed to stop when he

died. So much so that you would not accept his death, although he died from natural causes. So much so that you immersed yourself in natural medicines, exotic pharmaceutical compounds, and any and all computer gimmicks that helped you to fantasize about bringing your father back."

"No, Mother. That's not true. We're finished here, Madeline."

Ciaran stood again, grabbing Madeline's hand so that she would come with him.

"Did you or did you not create the computer character called White Knight?" Jennifer spat out the question.

"What?" Tadgh was astonished.

Madeline stared blankly at Jennifer, and then she turned around to observe Ciaran.

Jennifer continued, "You think your old mother knows nothing about what you do? You think you are in charge of the family, and I am living in oblivion in Dublin?"

"*Create*? So you are *the* White Knight?" Madeline asked, shocked.

"White Knight is a very critical and advanced program that could change the landscape of science, Madeline," Ciaran said.

Madeline stared at him. "I don't question your motives for creating such program. I am sure it will benefit humankind and more. But I *am* questioning your motives toward me. Did you arrange our *coincidental* meeting at Hyde Park?"

"No. I didn't know you before that."

"So did you know what I needed to do at our dinner?"

"Yes, but I only had general information. I didn't know your intentions."

"So that's why you let me into your headquarters so

easily. You wanted to scope me out!" Tears welled in Madeline's eyes.

"Madeline!" Ciaran approached, "It's not what it looks like."

"Why didn't you tell me you were *the* White Knight, Ciaran?"

"I . . . I didn't say I wasn't."

"It's the same as a lie. And I lied to you, too. We can't start a relationship based on lies. We aren't meant to be together, are we?" Tears were streaming down Madeline's face now.

"I would never tell a woman I worked with those programs. They're violent games. If she didn't know me, she'd think I was a serial killer," Tadgh chimed in and received a scolding glare from Jennifer.

Madeline stood up and headed toward the door. Ciaran grabbed her arms. "You said you'd give us a chance, Madeline. We need time." His voice was gentle but firm.

"Will you tell me everything? There can't be any secrets between us—" Madeline said.

"Everyone has secrets they can't share, no matter what," Jennifer cut in.

"Mother!" Ciaran growled, turning toward Jennifer.

"Let me help you elaborate on that, Ciaran. Can you honestly say that your wife did not die because of one of your secrets, Ciaran?"

"Juliette didn't die because of my secrets." Ciaran's voice quieted, but Jennifer could see the anger oozing from his pores. His eyes were red, and a vein on his forehead throbbed. She remained seated, staring at Ciaran while Tadgh stood.

"Perhaps not. Because she died *for* them. She robbed you of your heart, your life, and your secrets. She died for her greed," Jennifer continued.

"Why would you say that, Mother? Why do you hate me?" Ciaran flew in Jennifer's direction. Tadgh darted after him, but he was too slow. Ciaran punched the leg of a statue standing on a head-height column behind Jennifer. It cracked, crumbled, and collapsed to the floor. He braced his hands on the column, trying to suppress his anger.

Jennifer didn't even blink. She didn't need to look behind her to see Ciaran's expression because she could read that on Madeline's face. Madeline stepped back, tears rolling down her face. She turned around and headed toward the door.

Stephen entered the room just then and saw Madeline. He glanced at the scene before him and gently touched Madeline's shoulders. "Madeline, what's the matter?"

"I need to leave. Could you take me out of here, please?"

"You were attacked last night just outside this house. We have to be careful. We haven't found Jo. We could use some help."

"We found her. She got away yesterday and is with Detective Adamson. Please take me out of here. We can pick her up on the way."

"On the way to where? The car was trashed last night. Could you calm down? Stay here for a bit, and we can sort things out?" Stephen spoke gently.

"I can arrange transportation for you right now, if that's of any help." Jennifer's voice was as cold as steel.

"Lady LeBlanc, if you or your boys do anything to hurt Madeline, I will not let it slide," Stephen growled.

Ciaran turned his gaze from the ruined statue and directed it toward Stephen. Tadgh inched forward. Jennifer knew the sight of her sons would intimidate the hell out of Stephen, so she remained silent.

"They didn't hurt me or anything, Stephen."

"So why the hell do you look like this?"

"I just need to leave. Right now."

"Not until you tell me what happened. What did they do to make you cry?" Stephen threw a lethal stare at Ciaran.

"Nothing happened. It's my problem. Let's go get Jo and head back to New York. I don't belong here."

Stephen shook his head and stiffened his stance.

Madeline huffed out a breath. "Stephen, if you want to stay and pick a fight, feel free to do so—it seems there's enough testosterone in the room to do that—but I will leave here by myself."

The cheery sound of Mrs. Rutherford humming a country song as she pushed her teacart echoed into the room.

"Madeline, please stay a bit longer. The people who attacked you last night might still be out there waiting. If anything happens, I don't think I'm in any shape to help you."

Mrs. Rutherford entered the room, the aroma of her famous scones with jam and freshly brewed jasmine tea filled the room. She stood at the door and noticed the tension in the room right away, saw Madeline's tears.

"Morning tea, everyone." Her voice trembled a bit and sank into an awkward silence.

"Madeline . . ." Ciaran approached.

"Stay the fuck right there, Ciaran," Stephen yelled and stopped Ciaran in his tracks.

Madeline continued to head toward the door and had to step around the teacart.

"You, too! I said stay, Madeline!" Stephen growled.

Madeline took one more step and Stephen ran to her. He grabbed her shoulders violently and threw her back into the room. Madeline fell, rolling on the floor. Ciaran rushed to her, and Jennifer stood up from her chair.

Stephen grabbed Mrs. Rutherford, pulled out his gun, and pointed it at her head. "Stay still," he commanded the room.

Everyone froze.

"Lady LeBlanc, may I ask for your permission to stay thirty minutes longer at your palace?" Stephen asked, a sarcastic smirk on his face.

Ciaran inched closer to Madeline.

"I said, stay still, Ciaran. Or I'll put a bullet in her head." Stephen pressed the gun against Mrs. Rutherford's head.

"Stephen, what's going on?" Madeline asked.

"I wouldn't have had to do this if you'd behaved and done what I said. But you preferred to go about it the hard way."

"Let her go, Stephen. If I did anything to offend you, then take it out on me," Madeline pleaded.

"I would never hurt you, Madeline."

"I know you wouldn't. So let Mrs. Rutherford go. I'll do whatever you say. If you want me to stay here, I will."

"You will?"

"Yes."

"Liar!" Stephen screamed. "She's a stranger. She's nothing to you. I'm your *friend*, Madeline. Have you ever thought of me? Would you do anything for *me*?" Stephen's eyes sparked with insanity.

"You never asked for anything. If you'd asked, I'd have done anything for you." She tried to approach him.

"Stay right there." Stephen raised his gun, aiming at Madeline now. Tadgh and Ciaran rushed Stephen at the same time. Two gun shots discharged from the silencer on the gun muzzle, and both Ciaran and Tadgh slumped to the floor.

CHAPTER 39

The sound of the two bullets tore at her heart. Madeline turned around slowly. She knew Ciaran couldn't be dead, but she had to see with her own eyes. Ciaran and Tadgh pulled themselves up from the floor. A bullet had hit Ciaran's left shoulder and Tadgh's right leg. Madeline looked again at Stephen. He shrugged.

"I warned them to stay still." Stephen smirked. "I didn't mean to scare you, Madeline."

"Whatever it is that you want, we can talk about it. Let the women go," Ciaran said.

An insane peal of laughter came from Stephen. "Let the women go? What a gentlemen you are! So why didn't you give Juliette that chance?"

"Who the fuck are you?" Tadgh asked.

Stephen released Mrs. Rutherford, but still held on to her hair. "You don't even know your brother-in-law, Stefan? What kind of husband are you?"

"Juliette never mentioned your name. She must have been embarrassed by your very existence," Ciaran said with scorn.

"She told me enough. How do you think I knew about your technology and was able to get my weapon past it?"

Ciaran smiled. "It's obvious she didn't tell you enough. There is nothing here. You wasted your time and effort to get in."

"You think my sister married you for love?" Stefan laughed.

"What Juliette and I had, a scumbag like you could never understand. If she had married me for our family secrets, you wouldn't be here, threatening women to get what you want. You're pathetic!" Ciaran taunted.

Stefan angrily thrust the gun in Ciaran's direction. Madeline could see he was provoked enough to pull the trigger at any time. Despite the look of insanity on his face now, his eyes were still the same. They were still the eyes of the Stephen who fumbled his words whenever she smiled at him.

"What about *me*? What about *us*? Did you ever have any real feelings for me? I have nothing! I don't have any gold or secrets you could profit from." Madeline stepped toward Stefan.

Stefan's eyes softened a bit. "Of course I have feelings for you, Madeline. It took me years of digging around to find the last line of the Kelleys."

"Me? I'm a Kelley?" Madeline frantically searched in her head for a Kelley in her life. No, it rang no bell.

"Oh yeah! You're powerful when it comes to that. Don't you have any idea where your psychic ability comes from?"

"If you planned this whole thing, then tell me what you want from me."

"You got me inside Mon Ciel. That's all I needed."

"If that's all you needed, why bother with the kidnapping?"

Stefan laughed. "That was Zen's stupid idea. I paid him

to design the kidnap and create a scare big enough so that you would call for my help. But then he got fancy. He wanted the stupid hologame program and White Knight and all of that crap. He got tips from the wrong people and did everything *except* getting me what I'd paid him for. Then I had to pay someone else to get Jo off him so that he got nothing to give you at Rufford Abbey…"

Madeline cut in, "You wanted me to call you for help. I did. Now you are here, so do you want me to help you find the crucifix?"

"Oh no, sweetie, you stay right there. You're falling too deeply for that guy." He pointed toward Ciaran with the gun. "Just like Juliette. My feelings for you pretty much guarantee that I won't shoot you . . . unless you provoke me. Now, let's go and get the crucifix. You, come here." Stefan pointed the gun at Jennifer, waving her over.

"Oh, no, no! Don't do that to the lady," Mrs. Rutherford cried out. "Take me."

"Don't provoke him, Mrs. Rutherford." Jennifer walked toward Stefan.

"No, Mother." Ciaran and Tadgh walked toward Jennifer to stop her.

"Don't make me prove myself again!" Stefan yelled out.

"Please don't hurt the lady." Mrs. Rutherford charged toward Stefan. Madeline tried to grab her.

Stefan waved the gun. "Step back! Step back, you two."

A voice on the intercom announced, "Doctor Thomas has just arrived at the gate. He is on his way in."

Stefan was distracted momentarily, and Mrs. Rutherford charged toward the intercom corner and hit the panic button. Madeline tried to pull her back, but it was too late. Stefan fired his gun. The single bullet pierced Mrs. Rutherford's chest. She fell back into Madeline's arms, dead.

Alarm bells rang all over the building, and Madeline

deduced that it would alert the central security system and all related parties in the LeBlanc's security network.

Stefan laughed. He pointed the gun at Jennifer.

Ciaran and Tadgh stood up to protect their mother. But they stood at a distance, and Stefan could take them down, one by one.

Ciaran stepped forward. He looked as if he could grind Stefan into dust with his bare hands. Stefan pointed the gun at Ciaran. "Don't be foolish."

Suddenly it felt as if a whole army of security guards was charging toward the Great Reception. Madeline could feel the motion of many approaching people. She was sure Stefan knew it, too.

Jennifer cried out and slumped down, gasping for air. She was as white as a sheet. Ciaran ran over and held his mother. "She has asthma. She needs her medicine."

"I'll get it." Tadgh stood up.

"No one goes anywhere." Stefan waved his gun. "The faster you give me what I want, the faster she'll get her meds. Now come here."

"She can hardly stand Stefan," Madeline scolded.

"Then you ought to help her."

Madeline went toward Jennifer. "Can you hold up a little longer?" Jennifer was gasping but nodded. Madeline helped her up. "Now what?" Madeline asked.

"All right, the crucifix was in one of the statues. Given that you have so many in this house, where do you want to start? Be strategic, as Lady LeBlanc here doesn't look as if she can last long," Stefan said coldly.

"Right here, then," Ciaran responded.

The Great Reception was at the far end of the old section of the house. Madeline knew the old statues were marble or stone, and it would be really hard to hide anything in there. It would more likely be in the new extension of the house. Ciaran said it had been built around ten years ago. That must have been when he had married Juliette. So Ciaran was hoping to bide some time, Madeline thought. She took Jennifer to the chair.

"Well, then." Stefan signaled a go ahead. "Lead the way."

"What do you want me to do? Hammer the statues?" asked Ciaran.

"That won't be necessary. My little sister was a smart cookie. She would have tagged it with electronic chips. Do a scan. And do it carefully." He put his portable scanner on the floor and kicked it toward Ciaran.

Stefan was standing very close to Jennifer and Madeline, his back against the wall. That way, he had a full view of the entire room, the door, and the security team in the hallway.

The team apparently didn't know what to do, Madeline thought. She doubted Ciaran had had any time to replace Robert, and now with both Ciaran and Tadgh in this room, security clearly didn't have any leadership.

The warm and friendly voice of Doctor Thomas came across the room from the door. "Stephen, this is Doctor Thomas. I examined you this morning."

"Yes, I remember you. And it's Stefan. What do you want?"

"Could I please bring some water and medicine in for Jennifer, and check the bleeding on the boys' gunshot wounds?"

"Water and meds for the woman is okay. Nothing for the boys. Don't try anything silly, Doctor Thomas. See for yourself." Stefan nodded toward Mrs. Rutherford's dead body. Madeline could see the doctor's eyes waver with pity and sorrow for a fraction of a second, then he was calm again.

"Yes, Stefan. I can see clearly. May I come in now?"

Stefan waved his gun to signal Doctor Thomas to come in.

By the time they had finished scanning all the statues in the old quarter, the sun had begun setting, and the lights in the building had illuminated. They moved on toward the new quarter.

As soon as they entered the long corridor where the twelve statues stood, including the one with the missing toe, Madeline knew that what Stefan wanted was there. She shifted and felt the broken toe still in her jacket pocket. She swore to herself that if there was truly the spirit of a god in that statue, and if he helped her solve this disaster, not only she would put his toe back, but she would also name her first son after him.

The first statue Ciaran scanned resulted in a positive beeping signal. Stefan's face brightened. Ciaran slid his fingers along the edge of the marble base where the signal was the strongest. It was one solid piece of marble—no handle, button, or compartment of any kind. Then he stopped at a small copper plaque. That had to be it.

Stefan grabbed Jennifer and pulled her with him. Using a hunting knife, he gave the edge of the plaque a nudge. Nothing. He stabbed hard into the niche around the plaque until the copper piece gave way and dropped to the floor. Inside was a computer disc, neatly tucked away in plastic.

Stefan grabbed the disc and mumbled to himself. "What the fuck?"

"Do you want to read the disc?" Ciaran asked.

"You think I'm stupid? You want me to use your computer so you can copy it?"

Ciaran shrugged. "I'm curious, of course."

Stefan swung a hard kick at Ciaran's abdomen. Ciaran slumped to the floor, heaving in pain. His shoulder bled.

Jennifer cried out, "What else do you want? The crucifix apparently isn't here."

"I know!" Stefan screamed, giving Jennifer a hard push so that she fell into Madeline's arm.

Stefan pulled Ciaran up from the floor. As Ciaran was much taller than Stefan, he made a nice human shield. "I need to go now, and your master will escort me to safety." Stefan addressed the hopeless security team. "One wrong move from you, and he will eat my bullets. Now get out of my way."

The security backed off. Madeline could see that they have absolutely no idea how to handle the situation.

Stefan pulled Ciaran with him, backing out the door.

Madeline followed. "Stefan, you're a smart man, and you know better than anyone that your sister would have coded the disc, and that Ciaran might be the only person who can decode it for you."

Stefan laughed. "You've definitely fallen head over heels for this guy. You just don't want me to kill him, do you?"

"They were married, Stefan. You might not want to hear this, but their marriage was far more important to her than your brother-sister relationship. Otherwise, she would have given you the information. If she coded something in that disc, who do you thing she would let read it? You can barely turn a computer on."

"You'd better stop talking and stay right there."

"That's enough. You want to go, let's go," Ciaran cut in.

"I hate to repeat myself, but don't move. You won't like the consequences." Stefan threw out his last threat, addressing everyone, and pulled Ciaran away into a waiting car.

At the entrance of the house, Madeline watched as the car zoomed into the darkness. She heard a rumbling, chaotic movement behind her. Then there was a click and a humming sound, and a blue wave of light flashed outside and blanketed the entire Mon Ciel estate. Then the light disappeared, and Mon Ciel returned to its normal magnificence.

Jennifer cried out and slumped to the floor. Tadgh held his mother, a tear rolling down his face. Madeline could see his body shaking with emotion, but he tried to remain calm, perhaps to hang on to a thread of hope.

There was nothing in Jennifer's eyes but devastation.

Madeline approached and crouched next to Jennifer. In front of her was a desperate mother. "What was that blue light?" she asked, knowing that whatever the answer was, it wouldn't be good news.

"Ciaran put Mon Ciel in lockdown mode." Tears streamed down Jennifer's face.

Madeline frowned and looked at Tadgh.

"That means all weapons and machinery will be neutralized at the contact point outside the protective shield. No one can attack us from the outside," Tadgh explained.

"Can we take weapons out from the inside?" Madeline asked.

Tadgh shook his head. "You can't even drive a car out."

"Can you unlock it?"

Tadgh shook his head again. "Ciaran coded the lock. No one has access."

"Does that mean none of us can go out and help him if we need to?" Madeline asked.

"The shield doesn't stop human passing," Tadgh said.

They saw a flash flare up in the distant darkness and the sound of an explosion which was muffled by the thick foggy air. Jennifer was pale and numb with pain.

"I'm going after Ciaran," Madeline said and stood up.

"I'll go with you," Tadgh said.

"Not with that leg," Madeline snarled and strode to the kitchen. She grabbed a couple of knives and tucked them into her belt. When she returned to the hall, Tadgh had already patched up his wound. He had a combat knife tucked at his waist.

Seeing Madeline enter, Tadgh grinned. "If you can go out there in the dark on foot with those kitchen knives, I can do it with one good leg. Doctor Thomas patched up this stupid wound—and Ciaran's kick-ass painkillers will come in handy."

Madeline nodded. When she walked past, Jennifer grabbed her arm. "I'm in debt to you for this," she said. The tears had dried on her face, but the worry and exhaustion haunted her eyes.

"Ciaran went out to Fosse Way for me. This is the least I can do for him." She turned on her heel. Tadgh finished giving instructions to the troops staying behind, and then he followed Madeline out the door.

CHAPTER 40

*C*iaran clung to the steering wheel and focused on the dark road ahead. He could drive this road with his eyes closed, but at the moment, the more Stefan thought he was struggling, the better it was for him. Stefan didn't notice he had flicked on the protective shield to put Mon Ciel on lockdown. Those he loved would be safe inside the shield. Stefan wouldn't be working alone, and Ciaran wasn't sure how many he had left behind to attack Mon Ciel.

They were approaching the bridge over the creek where he had picked Madeline up this morning. He knew this creek well. Fast running water hit the rocks and created strange sounds that could sometimes be calming and therapeutic. But not now. Going down there with a bleeding wound on his shoulder was probably a dumb move, but it might be the only option he had.

Ciaran swung the steering wheel hard to lift the car over the rail. The bullet in his left shoulder was damn inconvenient. Instead of going over, the car smashed into the cement rail. The air bag assaulted his face and almost made him black out although he had anticipated the impact and turned sideways.

When the car grinded to a stop, there was no movement from Stefan. Ciaran unbuckled himself and exited the car, but before he could get to the other side to get Stefan's gun, strong headlights flashed at him. A truck and an armed group of men stood waiting at the bridge. They raised their guns and stopped Ciaran in his tracks.

From the passenger side of the car, Stefan emerged, rubbing his head. "Where the fuck have you been? I messaged you from the house!"

A man from the group stepped forward. "We didn't have a signal," he told Stefan.

Stefan pulled out a portable device and looked at the screen. "The gun works, but this piece of shit sure doesn't."

"Did you get what you need?"

"Not quite."

"So you still need him?" The man pointed his gun toward Ciaran.

Stefan shrugged. "Yes. Take him. Let's go." He walked toward the truck. Blood streamed from Ciaran's wound. He swayed and slumped to the ground. Stefan glanced back. "Take him with us. I need him."

The man nodded and approached Ciaran. But as soon as he touched Ciaran's arms, Ciaran jumped to his feet, stepped around him, and before he could do anything in retaliation, confiscated his gun. Ciaran stood behind him, using him as a shield, and pointed the gun at the man's temple.

Stefan turned back and cocked an eyebrow. "Only I use tricks like that, Ciaran. You think that will work on me?"

Stefan shot straight at the man's head. His brain splattered all over Ciaran.

Ciaran felt a force coming up from behind him and could see all the men standing next to the truck in front of him raising their guns. Stefan dove behind the truck. Ciaran swiveled to the side of the bridge toward the car.

The group of men behind him marched head on to those standing next to the truck. Guns discharged, and bullets sprayed from both sides.

A man behind him covered Ciaran. Bullets rained and punched holes in the man's body. He fell and squashed Ciaran to the ground. Men around him slumped to the ground like tree trunks. Ciaran heard the sounds of car tires squealing, and then everything went quiet.

He flipped the dead man on top of him over, steam still wafting from the bullet holes in his body. Ciaran observed a large hole in the man. "Wires," he muttered.

The thing on top of him was not a man.

Ciaran stood. There were about a dozen men-like beings in the group that had just rescued him. Before they could get too close, Ciaran hurled himself at the cement rail and threw his body over the bridge and into the rapids. If he wasn't mistaken, those men on the bridge were there to take him. *Thirty-three year cycle*, he thought. Was this the end of his human life?

His father had worked until the day he died to prevent this from happening. If this meant his death, he was fine with it. Everyone had to die someday. But his father had called this his *duty*—and he had said that he could deny it.

But what kind of duty? And if he had to go somewhere, what about his family here? And what about Madeline? She hadn't answered him when he'd asked if she would stay with him or go back to New York. He hadn't had a chance to explain to her that he had never meant to lie to her or hurt her in any way.

The icy water was pulling him with incredible speed,

freezing every blood cell of whatever blood he had left in his body. He saw a large clump of tree branches floating in the water. The force of the water was going to slam him into the tree branches, impaling his body on those giant claws. Ciaran used every ounce of his leftover strength and flipped his body sideways before he hit the branches.

The blow was like an explosion in his brain. He remained still for a moment, and then began to follow the tangle of tree branches to the bank of the creek. He slumped to the ground, trying to catch his breath and shivering with the cold. Then he felt a movement in front of him, and when he looked up, the group of men-like things from the bridge were surrounding him.

One of them spoke, "We're here to help you and mark your entry." Its voice was surprisingly human.

"Entry to what?" Ciaran's vision started to blur with his fatigue.

"Entry to the realm of righteousness and fulfilling your duty."

"Stop the bullshit. Who wants me? For what and where?"

Silence.

Ciaran chuckled. He wanted to laugh heartily but didn't have the energy to do so. In front of him stood a bunch of advanced artificial creatures with hardwired brains. His questions hadn't been previously programmed, so there was no way they could give him an answer.

"We are here to help you and mark your entry," the robot repeated.

"No. I reject your request." Ciaran used language that he speculated the robot would understand. "Go back to your commander and request him to contact me directly."

The eyes of the robot flashed as if processing the information. "We are here to help you and mark your entry," it repeated again.

Shit. This is their one-off mission. Ciaran turned to run but only made a couple of steps before he was surrounded. He felt a puncture at the back of his neck, and the world went black.

ith Tadgh trailing behind, Madeline ran in the dark, the bitter winter breeze slapping at her face and crawling under her skin. It might not be the chill but the fear of losing Ciaran that was clawing at her heart. She wanted one last chance to tell him she understood him, and that she was forever in his debt for going after her and protecting her at Fosse Way.

The moment the basket with four-week-old Madeline had landed in front of a random house, she'd had no protection from either those who had created her or those who raised her. Her soul was damaged. The thought that she was unwanted, and that she had been a mistake in this world had created a void in her that had never been filled.

Until, that is, she'd felt Ciaran's arms wrapped around her shoulders, protecting her from the bullets at Fosse Way. But it wasn't his heroic action that moved her. It was his genuine intent to protect her.

The man trusted no one. But in his most vulnerable moment during his rage, a flaw he wouldn't reveal to anyone, he had reached out to her. When their fingers had linked, when their hands were joined, she found the connection she had always longed for.

He filled her void. And somehow, she thought she filled his.

They approached the bridge, and the scene tore at her heart. Ciaran's car was severely smashed, crashed into the side of the bridge. But it hadn't gone over into the water. There were smear of blood, pools of red, and skid marks of larger vehicles. It looked like a war zone. But there was no sign of Ciaran.

Her heart thundered, and her blood boiled with fear. The winter air didn't seem cold anymore.

Where is he?

Tadgh was saying something, but she couldn't hear him. If her psychic ability was real and of any use, she needed it to work right now. But the signal was only strong if it was sent both ways. She could track him, but it might take forever, and it might not be accurate at all.

Help me, Ciaran, where are you? All you have to do is to think about me. Please!

And then it came. A flock of blue dots flashing at her from down the creek. She charged toward them as if her life depended on it.

There he was. Madeline saw the shape of his body sprawled on the ground. She trampled tree branches, rocks, and whatever poor wild animals were in her way. She hurried toward his body and knelt down. From the ground, Ciaran smiled up at her.

"Thank you for thinking of me. I couldn't do it without you," Madeline said to him while tears rolled down her face. She brushed the hair from his face. He was shivering, soaking wet, and there was blood everywhere.

She took her jacket off, but Tadgh pushed her aside. "Your jacket is just for show, Madeline." Tadgh took his thick coat off and wrapped it around Ciaran. "You've done a good job locking Mon Ciel down, Ciaran. Now we have no car, no chopper, and no men. Are you okay to stay here by yourself, Madeline? I'll run back to get more men to help carry him back."

"I can walk," Ciaran said weakly.

"Walk, my ass."

Ciaran tried to sit up, but he flopped back down and passed out.

"I rest my case," Tadgh mumbled and stood up to leave. Then they saw Mon Ciel's shield flash up in a brilliant blue light and turn off.

"Holy fu—," Tadgh muttered. "How you do that, Mother?" he asked the air.

The helicopter dispatched from Mon Ciel and, in a short moment, the search light swept over the spot where they were waiting.

CHAPTER 42

*M*adeline couldn't help it. She flew to the bed and panted a hard kiss on Ciaran's cheek as soon as he opened his smoky gray eyes. He smiled at her.

They heard a protesting moan from the corner of the room.

"He's jealous." Madeline grinned. "Come here!" She patted her hand on the bed next to Ciaran. From the corner of the room, the puppy darted forward and leaped onto the bed.

"This is TJ," Madeline said.

"TJ?" Ciaran asked, ignoring the dog sitting on the bed with his pink tongue poking out and his tail waving frantically.

"It's for traffic jam. Isn't it how you got him?"

"I didn't *get* him. He picked me because my car was the best looking one in the line."

"Is that right, TJ?" Madeline asked.

TJ lowered his head and snuggled against Ciaran's hip.

"Lily couldn't take care of him. She and her husband have a small apartment and are planning to have a family.

So if you don't take TJ in, he really will have to go to the pound."

"I'll ask Laurent."

TJ gave Ciaran his most pathetic puppy look.

"Come on, if the magnificent Mon Ciel can't accommodate a puppy, how can it accommodate me and my friend Jo?"

"Laurent's place is more appropriate. She has a yard and she loves . . . Wait, what did you just say?"

"I wondered whether Mon Ciel has room for me and Jo. I talked to her just a few hours ago. She's on her way to the London headquarters, and Lindsay will take her here."

Ciaran sat up. "TJ, I'll build you a doghouse, find you a girlfriend, and make sure you have plenty to eat for the rest of your natural dog life. Now, get out of the room—and close the door behind you."

TJ kept his puppy eyes fixed on Ciaran.

"That's all I can give you for now."

TJ licked Ciaran's hand then hopped off the bed and exited the room.

Ciaran held Madeline's hand and played with her long fingers. She interlocked her fingers with his.

"How long was I out?"

"Long enough. You're not in pain now, are you?"

Ciaran shook his head. "No. We make top of the line painkillers." He lifted his blanket and looked at his body—he was wearing nothing but bandages. Then he chuckled when he saw the smug look on Madeline's face.

"Sorry, I couldn't help it."

"Not fair," Ciaran said and pulled Madeline into his arms.

"I don't want to squash your injuries."

"I'll risk it." He kissed her.

"Seriously, Ciaran. You have cracked and bruised ribs,

three gashes on your legs, one on your right arm, and one on your back. I highly suggest that you limit the number of bullets you take in your left shoulder. Next time, switch to the other side."

"Thanks for the suggestion."

"Now, you might want to tell me how you seem to have left a war zone behind you on the bridge. How many men did you have to fight off to sustain the amount of injuries you've got, and among those you killed, was Stefan included?"

Ciaran winced when reality hit him, along with all of the issues he now had to confront.

"Stefan got away. And I didn't kill any men. There were two groups—one helped Stefan, and the other helped me. They canceled each other out."

"The group that helped you, are they the ones who gave you the tattoo?"

Ciaran frowned. Madeline peeled off a bandage on his left forearm, revealing a small tattoo of a crucifix.

The image glared back at Ciaran, another reminder of a brutal reality. Ciaran sat, leaning against the headboard. "Juliette and I shared a passion for alchemy. After we were married, she moved in here and started to work on a lot of alchemy-based medical formulas. Mother never trusted her. She said Juliette married me for reasons other than love."

Madeline laid her head on Ciaran's chest and kept their hands linked. He kissed her hair and stroked her back with his free hand.

"You loved her." She made a mental note but didn't realize that she had spoken out loud.

Ciaran nodded. He tilted Madeline's face up and looked into her eyes. "Yes, I love her and I always will."

"How did she die?"

"She was working on an important formula. She was confident, and I was young, foolish, and ambitious. She tested the formula on herself, and I didn't stop her. It didn't work. She died in my arms." His voice was hollow with the pain from the haunting past.

Madeline shifted and pushed Ciaran down to his pillow, kissing him lightly. "It wasn't your fault." She hoped her sultry voice melted into his mind and would have some soothing effect.

"It's a longer story than I care to tell. But she wouldn't have died if it wasn't for me. The most painful part was that Mother got the information that Juliette had taken a secret formula from our family and had hidden it in an artifact, a crucifix. I don't know where Mother got that information, but at the time, I didn't want to know—or believe it."

Ciaran tried to sit up, but Madeline held him down firmly.

"We scanned the house anyway and found nothing." Ciaran sighed and closed his eyes. "I later found a copy of our secret formula in the lab—that's the living proof of an attempt to duplicate it. My mother had been right all along. I never told her about what I'd found. But she always, despite the lack of evidence, believed that Juliette had an agenda in marrying me."

"And you love them both."

"What Juliette and I had was love, Madeline. I can't lie to you about that . . ."

Madeline covered his mouth with hers. She loved a man who knew how to love. If there wasn't any more room for love in his heart, then the current companionship they shared would be enough for her. . . Or maybe not. That last thought stopped her kiss and pulled a tear from her eye. It fell onto Ciaran's lips.

He swapped their positions so that she was beneath him. He gazed into her big brown eyes and rubbed his thumb at the dimple on her left cheek. "What I found in you is more important than the passionate love people have in their twenties. I don't know what you expect or look for in a relationship, but if the love that I had for Juliette is what you want, then I don't have that left in me."

Madeline tried to sit up, but Ciaran held her down firmly. He wiped a tear that escaped from her eye. "I can't speak for you. But let me be very selfish by telling you this. What I found in you is a missing part of me that I never thought I would find again. A part of me that I didn't even know I had lost. When I lost it, I simply didn't exist anymore. But now that part makes me whole. *You* make me whole."

She pulled him down to the bed so they lay face to face and traced her fingers along his jawline. "I've never been important to anyone."

"Then you start now." Ciaran pulled her toward him and devoured her lips. "Be a part of my life. Let me explore you." The sound came from deep in his throat. The words, the tone, and the meaning flew deliciously into her ears and into her soul as he whispered them. She reached up, kissing his throat, and at the same time, she yanked off her blouse.

He pleasured her jaw with small kisses, working his way down to her throat and then to her breasts. Her hands fumbled with the button of her pants, and she gasped and clawed at the bed sheet for purchase as he pulled them off in one swift move. His mouth assaulted her without mercy.

She hadn't been touched like this.

Hadn't been loved like this.

And hadn't been needed like this.

By anyone.

Every move he made was full of thought, care, love, and desire.

She was more than a woman. She was the one he needed.

And she was the one who reciprocated.

She flipped him over so she was on top of him. And what she had received from him, she gave back. And more.

More.

She locked her hands with his.

She was drunk in his pleasure as he did hers.

They moved in rhythm, in sync with their hearts and their minds. They took each other to another place that only they knew.

Their secret place.

~

A LONG WHILE LATER, Madeline nuzzled in Ciaran's arms, looking at the deep color of the feature wall and the elegant detail of the furniture in the room. She didn't want to stir as she might wake him. She loved to watch him sleep, to hear his heartbeat, and to feel the virility seeping out of his skin.

How long would this last? Hell, she didn't care. At the moment, she was on top of the world.

Ciaran's phone buzzed. She ignored it, but it had wakened Ciaran.

Damn!

Ciaran opened his eyes groggily and grabbed the phone. "Lindsay?" Ciaran's eyes switched to full alert mode instantly. He then grabbed the remote control and pointed it at the wall. The "wall" pulled up, revealing a gigantic screen.

On the screen was breaking news about Detective Adamson who had been killed in his own apartment.

Madeline's phone buzzed. She jumped off the bed and grabbed it.

"Jo?" Madeline gasped and held up the screen of her phone for Ciaran to see. There was no caller ID.

Ciaran shook his head. "It's not Jo. It's Stefan."

You have reached the end of Random Psychic.

You would know by now that the kidnap isn't the heart of the problem.

The disaster lies in the secrets Ciaran and Madeline keep. They keep secrets from themselves, from each other, and from the rest of the world.

If you love Random Psychic, Forever Mortal will excite you even more.

There will be more supernatural elements, more surprising twists and turns. And, it will conclude with an explosive ending.

>> **Turn to the next page for more information**

FOREVER MORTAL - CHAPTER 1

A drop of blood leaked from the center of the flower, ran down a petal, and dropped onto the wooden bench. The sound of it hitting the bench was in harmony with the raindrops tapping on the tin roof of the small shed.

Ciaran blinked.

The drop of blood vanished before his eyes.

"Ciaran!"

The voice came from Mrs. Hanson, an old gypsy, who approached him from behind. He almost jumped out of his skin. Almost. He cleared his throat, loosened up his tie and smiled. "Mrs. Hanson, I am here for the flowers."

"Certainly." Her smile was crooked. Ciaran thought she had probably been a mysterious and very beautiful woman before things had gone wrong with her alchemical practice. She had crossed the dangerous grounds of natural medicine and had paid a dear price. "I'll get the ribbons and wrap them for you."

Ciaran nodded in appreciation and returned to examine the flowers.

The purple strikes and swirls on the white petals of the Mountain Avens he had chemically engineered looked perfect. He understood why Juliette liked these wild flowers. They were plain, free, and determined, just like her spirit. He had created the purple strikes on the petals to make the flowers uniquely hers. Or maybe, to reflect her in his mind.

She had fallen in love with the flowers when they were on their honeymoon in Ireland over a year ago.

She'd intrigued him since the very first time they met. He was checking out a rare book in the library at Oxford University. She approached him, a total stranger, and asked if she could borrow a few dollars for a cup of pumpkin soup. Who could say no to her brilliant smile, magnificent flaming red hair, and eyes that contained a sea of innocence.

She did have a perfect explanation for asking. She wanted the soup. The shop was closing, so there wasn't enough time for her to run back to her dorm for the money. And after she got her soup, he walked her home to get his money back. At least, that was his excuse.

One thing led to another, and the next thing he knew, he married her despite his mother's objection.

"These flowers are cursed." Mrs. Hanson's voice interrupted Ciaran's concentration.

"I beg your pardon?" Ciaran had never raised his voice to Mrs. Hanson, or to anyone, but this statement not only demeaned his work and his belief in science but also his intentions to Juliette.

Mrs. Hanson shrugged as she wrapped a sheet of tissue paper around a pot of Mountain Avens and affixed a bow to it.

"I'm not a believer, Mrs. Hanson."

"Then you should start believing."

"You're wasting my time. What's the problem with the flowers?"

"You and Juliette are my good students. I don't want one of you to end up dead. I've been watching these flowers grow every day in my lab. They aren't normal. A couple of them turned red and bled drops of blood before they died yesterday."

"And you didn't think to let me know?"

"I'm letting you know now. You think I should have called your headquarters and wormed my way through an army of your minions just to tell you your little flowers died under tragic circumstances?"

Ciaran shrugged and pushed the pot of flowers away.

"So you don't want the flowers now? You believe me that they're cursed?"

"Of course I don't believe you. But you've said it now, and I don't feel comfortable giving them to Juliette anymore."

"Very well then. It's your decision." Mrs. Hanson smiled and turned on her heel to leave.

"Mrs. Hanson!"

"Yes."

"Never mind." Ciaran turned and strode out of Mrs. Hanson's little lab. There was no way in hell he was going to ask her whether the curse would still have an effect even if he didn't touch the flowers. *Ciaran LeBlanc is not superstitious,* he scolded himself.

He invented medicine that could change the landscape of science. He understood and accepted the fine line between science and fiction. He understood the human cognitive system and how theology worked on the human mind.

People had different beliefs. He could tolerate the differences. *But a curse? Hell no.* He wouldn't even mention it to Juliette because it was ludicrous. Juliette was a scientist.

He accidentally stepped on a bunch of wild daisies on his way out. As he moved his foot away, he saw trace of blood.

He jumped off the flowers, but the blood vanished right in front of him.

What the hell? He shook his head. He had been working way too hard in the last couple of weeks on a new project. It must be fatigue. Ciaran left Mrs. Hanson's house in a hurry.

He needed to go home.

*T*he familiar scent of vanilla and roses greeted Ciaran. He kicked his shoes off on the lush carpet of his master suite at Mon Ciel, the palace belonging to his family.

He might tell Juliette about the blood flowers. Whether or not he believed in superstition, what happened bothered him more than a little.

He pulled the tie from his collar and walked into the closet when a cool hand covered his eyes from behind. A voice as light and colorful as an Irish lullaby whispered into his ear, "Hello, stranger. My husband won't be happy at all when he finds out about you."

He turned around. "Your husband shouldn't be surprised. He married such a beautiful woman, he should know he's got competition."

He lifted her up. Juliette wrapped her long legs around his waist and let him carry her to bed. He lay her down on the bed and ravished her mouth. He hadn't seen her all day long—he was starved for her. He could comfortably justify it as the lust of newlyweds.

His hands stopped on her flaming red gown. She was wearing artfully applied makeup and her favorite perfume.

"Is there an occasion I have forgotten?" he asked, searching his mind frantically but coming up with nothing of significance attached to this particular day.

Juliette sat up, adjusted her hair, and smiled at him. "Do you like the dress?"

"Only if you wear it . . . and then take it off when appropriate . . ." He grinned.

He stood next to the bed, preparing for whatever might be coming at him. She still lay down, lazily rubbing her bare foot against his thighs.

"You've got to have an opinion about the dress as I'm wearing it to a very important function in a couple of weeks." She smiled.

Ciaran rolled his eyes and flopped face down on the bed. Juliette rubbed his back and wrapped her long legs around him. "I don't care what your forever-extended family will do for your birthday. But I have to have my private time with you. Also you have to open my presents before you deal with everyone else."

"I'm not dealing with anyone." His voice was muffled in the mattress.

"Darling, you're turning thirty. You've got to grow up at some point."

He sat up, leaning against the headboard. "This is my room, and you are my wife. That's all I want to know right now. I don't want to bring my family or anyone else into this bedroom."

She stood up. "And that's why we're celebrating your birthday here and now, just the two of us!"

He laughed. "It's a very attractive proposition. But it would be even better if you didn't wear any dress at all."

She winked. "I've got to wear something for you to take

off." She went to the wall cabinet and opened it. Inside was a tray with appetizers, a small birthday cake, champagne, and a small box wrapped in a bright purple ribbon. She poured champagne into some tall, slender glasses and brought them over to the bed.

She was stunning. He took his glass, still sitting on the bed, his eyes fixed on her face. He just wanted to ravish those lips that were made for sex. He hopped off the bed.

"No. You stay right there, birthday boy." She used a single finger to push him back to a sitting position on the bed. She climbed onto him and straddled his lap, facing him. As she gazed at him, he caught a brief glimpse of something strange in her eyes, but he was too distracted to dwell on it.

She drained her champagne. When he reached to kiss her lips, she stopped him. She yanked his shirt open and moved her lips to his chest. His pulse quickened, but just when his hands started to roam over her body, she whispered, "Let's look at your presents first." She put a small box in his hand.

He smiled and opened it. It was a small vial containing a clear liquid. He opened his mouth to say something, but she put a finger on his lips to stop his words. "You don't have to take it. But if your migraines turn bad, promise me you'll give this a try."

"Juliette!"

"Unless you don't trust me."

"You're one of the most competent engineers I've ever met. But I don't believe in Mrs. Hanson's natural medicines. I know you use her ingredients."

Juliette smiled. "I understand. And as I said, you don't have to take it."

He touched her cheek. "I don't want to disappoint you. Let's not argue over a headache medicine."

"What about something grander? Life, for example." She hummed the tune of a song she had written during their honeymoon, "Little hummingbird, do you see the sky? It is free. It is yours. Fly. Past the mountains. Past the oceans. There you will find love . . ."

"Juliette, what have you done?" He was beginning to understand the strange look in her eyes before. What he had seen was a shade of dark satisfaction. "Have you been working on the Golden Life?" he asked, knowing the answer already.

It was a project they'd started together before they got married—a medicine that could revive the newly dead. If successful, it would change the landscape of modern medicine. Only that would give Juliette this look of accomplishment.

"You have to be happy with this present, Ciaran. We've got it. We've made it. The Golden Life. I revived the lab rat. It didn't just come back as it was before—it was *better* than before death."

He had guessed the answer, but it still felt as if she had pulled the rug out from under him. "Are you out of your mind, Juliette?"

"You've worked on it your whole life, Ciaran. Why do you suddenly want to stop? Is it because it needs one ingredient you don't approve of?"

"And you've gone ahead and put it in apparently!" he could feel his rage coming. *Control*, he warned himself.

She smiled, a warm smile that was fading by the second. "You were right. That ingredient enabled the completion of the medicine. But it works. It's cruel, but it *works*, Ciaran." The smile had faded from her face, and she swayed. He caught her in his arms and carried her to the bed.

"Jesus Christ, don't tell me you tried it on yourself."

"Not yet."

"What did you take?"

She was almost out of breath. "My potion. There's nothing you can do, Ciaran. It was in my champagne glass." She smiled again.

"I can't believe you would do this to me, Juliette. Where's the damn drug?"

"In the cabinet."

He scrambled to the cabinet and saw another present dressed in purple ribbon. Opening it, he found a syringe in a box. He grabbed it and darted toward his wife.

Juliette lay in the bed, her eyes glassed over, but she still hummed her song. "Little hummingbird, do you see the sky?"

She grabbed his hand when he wanted to inject the medicine into her. "Not yet, Ciaran. If you do it now, it won't work."

"I can't wait until you die. I can't do that . . ."

"You have to. You should be happy, Ciaran, for what we have accomplished."

"I don't care . . ." He gathered her into his arms and rocked her. Regardless of whether he liked it or not, he knew she had to die for the medicine to work. She had to die so he could revive her. "Tell me you're not in pain, please . . ." he whispered.

"You were born to do this, Ciaran. You will change people's lives. You're a crusader."

"You don't know what it means to me, so don't say that."

"I know what it means to you. I know what it's like to do something that's larger than life. If I could be a part of your journey, I'll be happy."

"Please tell me you're not in pain . . ."

"I love you, Ciaran . . ." She closed her eyes and drew in her last breath.

He felt the vibration of emotion ready to burst out from him. His uncontrollable rage was coming. He was furious at himself and at the life's mission he'd set himself up with. He was angry it had caught up to the woman he loved. But there was no time to wallow in self-pity now. He held his breath and steadied his hands. He couldn't make mistakes now. He had to stay calm. He put Juliette down on the bed and checked the syringe. Then he injected the golden liquid into her.

He waited.

Ten seconds.

Thirty seconds.

Sixty seconds.

His head was pounding with a migraine, but he ignored it and concentrated on Juliette. There were no vital signs indicating she was coming back.

Stay calm! He stood from the bed and took the syringe. He would go to the lab, check the sample, and find the solution. He always found a way to get himself out of impossible situations. He had taken only two steps when the room exploded with light. Ciaran was thrown against the wall like a rag doll.

When he pulled himself up, he saw a man in his late fifties with flowing white hair, standing in a circle of white and blue light in the middle of the room. He looked quite formidable in his long black robe. "You killed her," said the man.

"No, I didn't. But if I don't get to the medicine, she will die."

The man looked Ciaran up and down. "I thought you were better than this. If it was possible to make the Golden Life, you would have made it."

The Golden Life was his deepest secret—only people in his family would know about it. His mind raced hundreds of possibilities why this stranger knew his secret. But he had to tend to Juliette. "I have to get to the lab!" Ciaran rushed toward the door.

An invisible force grabbed at him and threw him to the wall again. "No point. She's dead, and that's your fault."

The man stared at Ciaran. The man didn't making any physical movement except for a slight narrowing of his eyes. The invisible force squeezed around Ciaran's neck, choking him.

"Air bending. Who are you?" Ciaran gasped for air.

The man smirked. "You're knowledgeable, Ciaran, but not enough to save yourself."

The migraine was nothing compared to the pain the force was causing him right now. His life was drifting away from him. "Who . . . are . . . you?"

"Mon Ciel isn't as safe as your mother thought. All I need is a channel to get in here." The man narrowed his eyes even more, and the force squeezed harder at Ciaran's neck and crushed his body. Then Ciaran heard the door burst open. People stormed into the room. There was the sound of a gunshot and a struggle.

And then he didn't remember anything else.

A SHADE OF MIND
by D.N Leo

RANDOM PSYCHIC
FOREVER MORTAL
ELUSIVE BEINGS
IMPERFECT DIVINE

>> click here to get FOREVER MORTAL<<
(or go to http://dnleo.com)

>>>SERIES HOME PAGE<<<

Random Psychic
A Shade of Mind
Book 1